The Black QUEEN

TO BRENDAN —

SOME THINGS COME CLEAR QUICKLY — OTHERS TAKE TIME —

ON The Hunt,

[signature]

2003

Text set in Palatino
Copyright 2003 by Robert Holland
Printed on acid-free paper in Canada
ISBN 0 -9720922-1-8

Cover and title page illustrations and design by
Kirk Roberts

Frost Hollow Publishers,LLC
411 Barlow Cemetery Road
Woodstock, CT 06281
phone: 860-974-2081
fax: 860-974-0813
email:frosthollow@mindspring.com
website: frosthollowpub.com

The Black QUEEN

A Novel of Mystery and Adventure

BY Robert Holland

FROST HOLLOW
PUBLISHERS, LLC
Woodstock, Connecticut

More
Books for Boys
By
Robert Holland

The Voice of the Tree
The Purple Car
Summer on Kidd's Creek
Footballs Never Bounce True
Breakin' Stones
Eben Stroud
Harry the Hook
Mad Max Murphy
The One-Legged Man Who Came Out of a Well
The Last Champion
Charlie Dollarhide

Other Fiction by Robert Holland:
The Hunter
Things Got in the Way
Conversations With a Man Long Dead

Check your local bookseller or order directly from Frost Hollow. Call toll free at 877-974-2081.

The books for boys are $10.95 except for *Harry The Hook*, which is $12.00. Shipping and handling and CT sales tax extra.

Things Got in the Way and *Conversations With a Man Long Dead* are $17.95.

Also check out our web site at frosthollowpub.com. Read about the books in the series and find out what's coming next.

1

Out Of A Summer Sky

The only thing that had gone right since Aaron had turned ourteen in the spring of 1948 was having suddenly grown aller than his mother. But even that wasn't such a big deal ecause she was only five-six and his father had been six-wo and he wanted to be at least that tall. Even just six feet vould be okay. Not great. Just okay.

And as if that wasn't enough to worry about, he would e starting high school in September, and he had no idea vhat kind of nasty stuff might be waiting for him there, never nind how much harder he was going to have to work. He ould deal with having to work, but he wasn't so sure about he high school itself, mostly because it was so big, fifteen undred kids in one building. He set the thought aside, if only because there was nothing he could do about it. In September he'd get on the bus and go to school because that's what you did. But at least if he was at home he could've talked to his friends about it, and instead he'd been jerked away to spend the last month of the summer in a spooky old house that had neither electricity nor running water and looked like the only things that had lived in it for a hundred years were ghosts. He wasn't much in favor of ghosts. Not that he'd ever seen one, but he'd heard enough stories to convince him that such things existed and if ever he'd seen a haunted house it was the one his mother had rented.

Clay, who was two years younger, thought the whole thing was neat, but then he always liked new things, going to new places. He was even excited about starting junior high school because they had a football team and the fact that the eighth graders were bigger didn't bother him at all. The only thing in the world that Clay feared was spiders, which, when you thought of all the other scary stuff, seemed ridiculous.

Look at what I'm facing, Aaron thought: high school where the guys in the upper grades were all a whole lot bigger. It might even mean he'd have to fight and he'd had enough of that in the neighborhood. Besides, Clay always saw the good side of things. So did his mother. And then, again, as he did so often, he wondered what his father would have thought. Try as he might, he would never know that. He wished he'd been older when his father had been killed in the war. At least then he would have known him better.

Because it was Clay's turn in the front, he sat in the back seat of the car and gazed out the window at the unfamiliar landscape; the scrubby pines and oaks on one side of the road and an endless marsh on the other, trying to find at least one good thing about this vacation to Cape Cod.

Okay, he could think of one thing. They probably wouldn't get polio, and just now, at home in the humidity and heat and with a lot of kids around, that was a risk. It was why they were here. And then he thought of another benefit of being here. The beach. He loved going to the beach. He liked the sand and the salt water and searching through the shallow water and tidal pools for the critters he had seen pictures of in books. And he liked to swim and build castles in the sand. What he didn't like was the crowds, and the beaches they went to at home were always crowded.

So it was a surprise when he saw no other cars in the small parking lot, which was hardly more than just a wide sandy spot at the end of the road. They pulled the beach gear from the car and walked off onto the hot sand. The tide was out, and patches of eel grass grew here and there between the sand flats, but that wasn't what surprised him.

"There's nobody here," Aaron said.

His mother smiled. "It's why we came so far."

"To get away from the polio," Clay said.

"I never saw a beach without any people! We can build all the sand castles we want and there's nobody to knock them down." Aaron looked around at his mother, aware as always now, that he was taller by two inches. "Can we go swimming?"

"Of course."

With a whoop he headed for the water with Clay right behind him. Maybe this wouldn't be so bad after all. Together they walked over the rippled sand flats and then through the ankle-deep water, and then they walked a long way before it got deep enough to swim, and even then it was only waist-deep on Clay. Through the clear water they could see the sandy bottom rippled like ribbon candy by the waves. Above them, herring gulls and terns soared, their calls sharp in the soft breeze from the water.

From where they stood, looking back at the shore, way off to the left they could see several cottages along the high bluff and below on the beach an occasional brightly colored beach umbrella. And then, where the cottages left off, the bluff ran a long way back toward them without a single house or cottage and the beach below lay deserted.

For awhile they frolicked in the warm water, diving and splashing and when they grew tired of that, they headed back to the beach for a round of sandcastles and books and sun tan oil. Both boys had fair skin and blond hair cut summer short, but they tanned well once they got past burning, and because this was August they were both well tanned.

At fourteen, Aaron should have been the leader, and in some ways he was, but Aaron had never cared about being in charge. He preferred taking care of his own business. But if he did not choose to lead, he also disliked being led.

Suddenly, in the distance they heard the unmistakable deep drone of fighter plane engines and they looked up, staring off to the northwest at a group of Hellcats flying in tight formation, coming in high off the water, four of them, maybe a mile out to sea, swooping in on what looked to them like a helpless freighter. Even from that distance they could see the machine guns open up and then came the sound of the guns and then they could see where the bullets hit the water. Each plane made a single strafing run and then the engines throbbed in the summer air as the planes rose upward, wheeled, and dove back down at the ship to drop their bombs.

The explosions made bright yellow and orange flashes and the booms followed, flat dull thuds rolling across the water. Only one bomb hit the freighter and then the planes rose higher, resumed formation, and headed back the way they had come, shrinking in size until they disappeared into the distant clouds.

Both boys ran for the beach. "Did you see that? Mom, did you see that?" Clay shouted. "Real guns and bombs!" He turned to his older brother. "Did you see that, Aaron?"

"It was amazing!" Aaron said.

"Wow! I never thought I'd see anything like that!" Clay couldn't stay still, walking back and forth and looking out at the freighter which, surprisingly, seemed undamaged. He had expected to see it burst into flames and then slowly sink out of sight into Cape Cod Bay. "At first I thought it was just a regular ship."

"It's just target practice," his mother said.

"Who cares! Boy, would I like to fly one of those planes!" He swooped his right hand through the air, imitating a fighter. "Whroom ... pow!" He ran in circles on the sandy beach, his arms extended, howling and imitating the sound of the planes and the machine guns and the bombs. Finally, he dropped back down onto the blanket. "Do you think they'll come back?" he asked.

"Mr. Watson, at the store, said they come in several times a day," his mother said. She adjusted herself in her beach chair and went back to reading her book.

"Com'on, Aaron, let's go back in the water."

"Don't go out too far," their mother said.

"Okay," Aaron said.

Just a short way out, in the shallow water, Aaron spotted a large dark shape crawling across the bottom. It was a horseshoe crab and it was the first time he'd ever seen one alive. Before he'd seen only the dried-up shells. And then without thinking he called to his brother. "Clay, you gotta see this!" He followed the crab along through the shin-deep water.

Clay came up alongside. "What is it?" he asked.

"Horseshoe crab, isn't it neat?"

"Do they bite?"

"Naw, but you don't want to step on its tail. If you stepped on it, it'd go right through your foot."

"Really?"

"Sure, look at it. It's just like a spike."

"What does it look like underneath?"

"Just a lot of legs."

"Legs? What kind of legs?"

"Not like a spider, if that's what you're worried about."

"I'm not afraid of spiders any more," Clay said, though he didn't think Aaron would believe that.

"Good. There's nothing to be afraid of." He plunged forward, and closing in on the hapless crab, drove his hand down into the water, caught hold of the tail and pulled it up into the air, the water flying away with all the legs flailing and flapping. Then he turned toward the beach. "Hey, Mom, look! I caught a horseshoe crab!"

Clay took one look at all those legs thrashing in the air

and all he could think of was a spider, but not just any spider … oh no … this was the world's biggest spider. "Let it go!"

"What's the matter, you afraid of an old horseshoe crab?"

"No! Just let it go …"

Aaron dropped the horseshoe crab, letting it fall with a splash back into the water. "There's nothing to worry about, Clay. They're harmless."

"What about the other kinds of crabs?"

"The only thing they can do is pinch you."

"How do you know?"

"I read about it in a book I got from the library. It was all about the stuff you can find in salt water. The only nasty thing is jellyfish. They sting you and it itches like poison ivy."

"Jelly fish?" Clay asked. It sounded like something Aaron had made up just to scare him. Jelly fish? How could a fish be made out of jelly?

"They just float around on the tide and currents and they have long tentacles and when a fish swims into them, they sting the fish and paralyze it, and then they eat the fish."

In his mind Clay made a picture of something big enough to paralyze a fish. "They got jelly fish here?"

"Sure. They're everywhere in saltwater. Don't you remember two summers ago when Uncle John rented a cottage and we went to visit and we dug clams? Remember him telling us to look out for the jellyfish?"

"I only remember the clams."

"Well, he told us about the jellyfish but we never saw any. There's even a really big jellyfish called a Portuguese Man O' War. They have enough poison to kill you, but you don't see them this far north, usually."

Clay began searching the water. Some of his friends' brothers would make up stuff like this just to scare them, but Aaron never did that. In fact, as brothers went, Aaron was the best older brother he knew. He even let him tag along with the older guys and nobody else had a brother who did that. What's more, Aaron read all the time and he remembered everything he read, especially anything about science, so when he told you about something like jelly fish, there was no reason not to believe him.

The sudden blast out at sea startled them both and then they stood, watching as another group of planes made their run. One after another the planes swooped in, dive bombing as they roared out of the clear sky, then rose up, circled, and dove back in at the freighter, machine guns blazing as they strafed the old hulk. And then one of the planes suddenly veered toward the land, smoke pouring out of its engine.

Aaron and Clay turned and ran through the water toward the beach, glancing back at the plane coming steadily closer, and it seemed to be coming right at them.

"Run! Run!" their mother shouted at them from the beach, pointing off to the left.

"Go left!" Aaron shouted and Clay turned with him and they ran to the left, came up onto the sand flat and now with the water no longer dragging at their legs they tore across the flat, not daring to look as they heard the plane screaming through the air and then it went past them well off to the right and they turned to watch it come down, the pilot keeping the nose up so the plane landed on its belly and went skidding across the shallows, throwing enormous sheets of water on both sides as it nosed on into the eel grass of the marsh. Even before it stopped, the pilot pulled himself out of the cockpit and leaped away from the plane, running as fast as he could, lifting his legs high to clear the grass and the water and just then the plane exploded and he dove down onto his stomach as pieces of the engine cowling flew through the air over his head.

The bright orange fireball rose up into a dense cloud of black smoke and then the fire seemed to settle into a steady burn. The pilot got up and ran toward them, hollering as he ran. "Get away! Get back as far as you can!" They turned then and ran down the beach, the boys angling in toward the shore and their mother running straight down the beach. And now the pilot had reached solid ground and he ran as fast as he could, heading for the point where a finger of the sandy bluff stuck out into the beach and he pointed toward the bluff and shouted, "Get behind there! Get behind there!"

All four of them reached the bluff and then ducked behind it at almost at the same instant and that's when the gas in the remaining fuel tank went off. The explosion seemed to tear apart the air and parts from the plane flew in all directions. From behind the bluff they watched pieces of metal zip past, whistling in the air, and then suddenly it was quiet and they looked out around the bluff at the remains of the plane, the orange fire leaping high into the air.

The pilot pulled off his soft helmet, and smoothed his rumpled dark hair. "You okay?"

"I ... I think so," their mother said. She looked around at her sons who stood with eyes wide open, still too astonished to speak. "You guys okay?"

They both nodded.

"Sorry I came so close," the pilot said. "Without my engine all I could do was try to keep the nose up." He wiped a hand across his face, smearing the soot from the fire in the engine. He smiled. "I'm Eddie Bayles."

"Linda Harrison, Captain," their mother said, "and these are my sons, Aaron and Clay." They shook hands.

"Sorry to drop in so unexpectedly," Captain Bayles said.

"It certainly was a grand entrance," Linda said. "I can't believe you got out of it."

"I'd have used my chute but I couldn't get any altitude after the fire broke out. All I could do was ride it down."

In the distance they could hear the fire sirens.

"That was even better than the movies," Clay said.

"We're all pretty lucky," Captain Bayles said. "The starboard fuel tank went first and it was mostly underwater. If the other one had gone first none of us might be standing here. I'm just glad I'd already dropped my bomb. That would have made things really exciting."

"Is this why they call it First Encounter Beach?" Aaron asked, and his mother and Captain Bayles laughed.

"It was an amazing landing!" Linda said.

"I was lucky. Just lucky. It could have blown up at any time." He shook his head. "Sometimes, I guess, God truly is riding copilot."

They watched the fire truck pull up and then they turned and started walking toward the smoldering wreckage.

"What made the engine catch fire?" Aaron asked.

"Good question. The only time during the war I had to bail out was when I got caught between two Zeros and one of them got a machine gun round into the engine. All I got was wet." He shook his head. "Today was a lot like that."

And then Captain Bayles went off with the firemen and cops and they sat on the blanket and just watched.

"I don't know whether you know it or not," their mother said, "but not just any pilot could have landed that plane and gotten out of it. I think Captain Bayles must be an exceptional pilot."

"It happens all the time in the movies," Clay said.

"A lot of things happen in movies," Linda said, "but that doesn't make them real."

Clay was having none of it. "But how can they take pictures of something that doesn't happen?"

"They have lots of tricks, Clay," she said. "Remember, seeing is not always believing."

Maybe, Aaron thought, this wouldn't be such a bad vacation after all, though he couldn't think of what else could be nearly as exciting. And then as he looked around, he saw a short, gray-bearded man standing high up on the bluff watching the activity below. He was dressed in work clothes, blue jeans and a short-sleeved blue shirt and he stood with his arms crossed.

Slowly, he turned his head and looked directly at Aaron, held his gaze for several seconds, and then he seemed to drift downward, as if he were settling into quicksand.

Aaron looked away from the bluff, wondering why the man had moved off out of sight. Had he just changed position so he could see better? Had he seen enough and simply left? Either explanation would do, and anyway, it didn't matter.

2

Whose Beach Is This?

While the firemen pumped water onto the wreckage
the plane, the police talked to Captain Bayles, and Lin
made the boys put on their sneakers because of the dang
of cutting their feet on the rubble from the plane. She got
argument. Right now, arguing wasted time.

Every piece they found that was small enough to car
they brought down to the parking lot where the firemen h
begun piling up the debris. It was a great game, but it g
truly exciting when they found a piece of the engine cov
ing, a piece too big to carry, and Aaron rolled it over a
discovered an odd hole in the metal.

"Holy cow," he said, "look at that!"

"What?" Clay asked.

"That!" He pointed to the hole.

"So what?"

"It looks like a bullet hole, that's what!"

"How would you know what a bullet hole looks like?"

"From the movies. That's just what it looks like when a bullet goes through metal."

"Sometimes you're full of it, Aaron, you know that?"

"Okay, you don't believe me? I'll ask Captain Bayles."

They turned and walked off to where Captain Bayles stood talking to one of the policemen, waiting politely until the conversation paused and when it did, Aaron spoke.

"Captain, could you come over and look at something we found?"

He grinned. "Sure." He turned to the policeman. "Excuse me for a second, will you, officer?"

The policeman nodded and Captain Bayles turned and followed them down the beach toward the water.

"Now what have you guys found that's so urgent?"

"We just wanted you to see this and tell us what it is."

Captain Bayles smiled, deciding it was best just to go along and help calm these guys down.

"There," Aaron said and he pointed at the rounded piece of metal. "What is it?"

"It's a piece of engine cowling, that's the metal that surrounds the engine."

Aaron pointed to the hole. "I told Clay that was a bullet hole, was I right?"

Captain Bayles squatted down and looked at the slightly oval hole, the edges rounded inward. He ran his finger around it and then looked out to sea toward the freighter and shook his head. "Boys," he said, "I think you'd better keep quiet about this."

"Then I was right," Aaron said.

"I can't be certain, but I saw enough bullet holes in metal during the war to have a pretty good idea. And I know that hole wasn't there when I took off. I'll have to get an expert to look at it."

"Did somebody shoot down your plane?" Clay asked.

"Offhand, I'd say that's exactly what happened." He stood up and looked down at them. "That's why you can't say anything."

"Even to our mother?" Clay asked.

"You can tell your mother, but no one else. A thing like this is a military secret, you know."

They started walking toward the blanket.

"Where did the piece of cowling go … on the plane, I mean?" Aaron asked.

"Pretty sharp question, there, Aaron," Captain Bayles said. "Once you know that and the direction I was flying, you can begin to guess at where the shot came from, right?"

Aaron smiled. "Sure," he said.

"Well, to tell you the truth, I'm not sure. I just fly the planes, I don't build them. But Grumman will know."

"Who's Grumman?" Aaron asked.

"The company that built the plane." He looked around as if expecting to catch someone watching. In fact, there were a whole lot of people watching; people from the cottages farther down the bluff, and more people had driven down to the beach, causing a major traffic jam. "In fact," he said, "I'll bet any one of our mechanics can tell me."

Out in the bay a Coast Guard cutter had pulled up and dropped anchor, and now a crew of four in a smaller boat driven by an outboard were headed toward the beach. The tide, which had been coming steadily in, had gotten high enough to allow them to bring the boat all the way in to the beach. The first man ashore was a lieutenant, the captain of the cutter. He walked across the sand to where Captain Bayles stood, and saluted.

"Captain, I'm Ensign Jim Walker. We've been in touch with the people from your base and they're on their way in a seaplane with a full crew to take charge here. In the meantime I've been directed to take charge of the area and …"

"Well, Ensign, I think you'd better talk with the firemen and the cops first, don't you? In fact, let's both of us go talk to them."

"Thank you, sir. My orders are to keep civilians out of the area until the seaplane arrives."

Captain Bayles shook his head. "I don't want to interfere with your orders, Ensign, but I think it might be best to just let things run their course here without undue interference. No sense in getting people all excited over nothing, is there?"

"With all due respect, Captain, my commanding officer, Commander Cartwright, was particularly clear on this."

"And with all due respect to Commander Cartwright, I'm the senior officer here and I'm going to assume command of the situation. What I need is to have your men begin combing the beach and the marsh for any pieces of the plane they can find and then bring them over to the parking lot. It would help if you made an announcement, advising people that it would be good to stay clear of the area until any unexploded munitions have been accounted for."

The ensign smiled. "Yes, sir. But Commander Cartwright isn't going to like this."

"It's my responsibility, Ensign."

"Yes sir." He saluted again and moved off to carry out his task.

The mention of munitions had the desired effect and people began moving back and the cars began to thin out, until only the Coast Guard, the firemen, the police, and the Harrisons were left.

They sat well apart from the plane, watching closely.

"Do you really think he was shot down?" Clay asked.

"Sure," Aaron said. "You saw the bullet hole."

Clay, squinting in the bright sun, turned toward his mother. "Do you think he was shot down, Mom?"

"I'm not sure what to think," she said. "Why would anyone do such a thing?"

"A spy," Aaron said.

"But the war's been over for three years," his mother said.

"Well, how would I know?" Aaron asked. "Maybe it was an accident. Or maybe it was one of those Communists!"

"But where would the shot have come from?" his mother asked.

Aaron looked out to sea at the old ship that had been scuttled onto a reef for target practice. "I bet it was somebody on the target ship."

"How would they get out there?" Clay asked.

"In a boat, you idiot."

"Don't call your brother names," Linda said.

"Yeah, Aaron, and besides, the planes would have seen

the boat."

"Sorry, Clay," Aaron said. "I didn't think about them seeing the boat."

Clay grinned.

"You know what I think?" their mother said. "I think it's time to go take a swim in that pond up the road to wash off the salt and then go home and start fixing supper."

"We have to wait for the seaplane!" Clay said. "We can't miss the seaplane!"

No sooner had he spoken than they heard the drone of aircraft engines and looked around to watch a big two-engine seaplane drop onto the water and taxi toward the beach. It came a long way in, but still stopped well out from shore and the Coast Guard went out to meet them in their boat.

As soon as the men from the seaplane stepped onto the beach, everything changed. There were two officers and ten men and while the seamen began sorting through the pile of debris, arranging the pieces as if they were building a plane right there on the parking lot, the officers walked off with Captain Bayles. They also sent the firemen and police away and then one of the officers walked over to the blanket. "Good afternoon, Ma'am," he said, "I'm Commander Grass, and I'm afraid I'll have to ask you to leave until we can complete our investigation."

Linda stood up and looked at him. "Of course, Commander." She turned to her sons. "Okay, guys, grab your stuff." She turned back to the tall officer. "How long is this likely to take, Commander?"

"I can't say, ma'am. A couple of days I shoul…"

"Now, just a minute, Commander. This is a public beach

and we're here on vacation. Are you saying we won't be able to use the beach for two days?"

"Those are my orders, ma'am."

"Well, I think perhaps you ought to check those orders again, Commander, because we will be using this beach every day."

For the boys it was like watching a tennis match, and they were astonished to hear their mother standing up for their rights.

"I'll be sure to check them," he said.

"Good. I understand you have a job to do, but after all, it was your plane that caused the problem. And I certainly don't understand why you would need to close down the entire beach, or even under what authority."

"Yes, ma'am."

"My husband was an Academy graduate. Commander Winslow Harrison. You may have heard of him. I mention this because I want you to understand that I know a great deal about what the Navy can and cannot do in such matters."

"Yes, ma'am."

Aaron and Clay stood absolutely thunderstruck at their mother's courage. Here she was, facing an officer and not backing down one inch, and now there was a sudden change in the Commander.

"Would you please do that now?" their mother asked.

"Yes, ma'am."

He nodded, turned, and walked across the beach to where Captain Bayles stood talking to another Navy captain and the Coast Guard lieutenant. He said something to them and then Captain Bayles and the other senior officer turned and walked back toward them as they finished gathering their things.

"Mrs. Harrison," Captain Bayles said, "this is Captain Franklin."

"How do you do, Captain," she said.

"Ma'am."

"You've talked to your commander, then?" she asked.

"Yes, and I'm afraid he's right. It's pretty much standard procedure whenever a military plane goes down."

She pointed down the beach which stretched for miles. "But how can you close the entire beach?"

"It's standard procedure until we close our investigation, Mrs. Harrison."

"Captain, I can certainly understand closing off the area where the plane went down, but it seems somewhat excessive to include the entire beach."

Captain Franklin had not expected an argument. He gave orders and people carried them out. How he hated having to deal with civilians. He glanced over at Captain Bayles but saw no help coming from that quarter.

"Captain, I certainly don't want to make a federal case out of this, but I think it's perfectly reasonable for us to go on using the beach. It really is quite a large beach and we take up very little room. But we'd be glad to move farther down the beach, if that would be any help."

He sighed, took off his cap, wiped away the sweat with his handkerchief and then replaced his cap. "Yes," he said. "I suppose it's really just the area where the plane went down. We worry, of course, about anyone stepping on something sharp and we would ask that any pieces of the plane you should happen on be returned so we can get on with our investigation."

"Of course." She smiled. "I think this will work out nicely. We'll stay to the area beyond the bluff. Will that do?"

"That will do nicely."

"Thank you, Captain."

He smiled. "It's an honor to meet you, Mrs. Harrison. Your husband was one of my heroes, and the best sub skipper we had."

"Thank you, Captain," Linda said and then she smiled. "It helps to hear such things."

Not until they were back in the car did either boy say anything, and it was Aaron who spoke first. "That was amazing, Mom," he said.

"What was?"

"The way you talked to all those officers."

"I wasn't about to let them ruin our vacation."

"In the movies nobody talks to officers that way," Clay said.

"Well, remember, you two, that my father is a doctor and my grandfather was a lawyer and Uncle Nolan is a judge. Nobody in my family backs down, especially when they know they're right."

"I thought Navy officers could, I mean, I thought they were in control," Aaron said.

"They are in things that are military. And Captain Franklin was only doing his job. But we have a right to use that beach and I wanted them to know that."

"Dad must have been a great hero," Aaron said.

"He was, Aaron. And he was a great man."

"I want to be just like him," Clay said, adding quickly, "except that I want to fly planes. I don't think I would like being in a submarine."

"I would," Aaron said. "I like going underwater. I'd like to see what's in the deepest parts of the ocean."

"You don't have to join the Navy to find that out," their mother said. "You have to go to college and study." She smiled. "Besides, you can't see out of a sub when it's underwater."

"You can't?"

"They don't have windows because of the pressure of the water."

She pulled in at the fresh water pond and they jumped out, ran down, and dove in. The crystal clear water was cool and they swam back and forth and then when they got close to the beach, their mother produced a bar of soap and all three of them lathered up and then rinsed off. It was simply what you did in the summer when you were living in a place that had no running water.

"Hey, Aaron," Clay said, "you wanna play battleships when we get back to the cottage?"

"Okay," Aaron said. Clay loved games of any kind and he was very good at all of them, except chess. Aaron would rather have played chess, but there would be plenty of time for that, and anyway, he truly did like playing battleships.

He smiled to himself. This vacation was definitely looking up. After all, how many guys did he know who went on vacation and had a Hellcat nearly drop into their lap?

3

A Trip To The Store

The next morning Clay, as he always did, got up early, and immediately an ugly problem surfaced. He had to take a leak and that meant using the outhouse, which meant he stood a good chance of running smack into some monster spider. On the other hand ... he didn't have a lot of choice.

Quickly, he shucked his pajamas and pulled on his shorts and sneaks and headed downstairs and outside, trotting toward the outhouse. Ten feet away he stopped. The small building, with its sickle moon in the door, looked decidedly unfriendly. Inside it would be dark and damp. Perfect spider country. Big, nasty spiders. He shivered.

He looked around quickly. Heck, he didn't even have to use the outhouse. All he had to do was stay behind the house so he couldn't be seen from the road. He unbuttoned his fly and took care of business, looking now at the marsh and how close the high tide brought the water to the back of the house. Now he could see channels through the marsh that didn't show at low tide because they lay hidden by the tall eel grass.

As he stood there, he felt suddenly as if someone were watching him and he looked over his shoulder to the left and then to the right. Nothing. Not even a sound except for some crows and gulls in the distance. He looked again to his left at the big old barn that stood some fifty feet from the house. He shivered once, buttoned up his shorts, and walked toward the barn, drawn as surely as if some unseen power were dragging him forward.

And then, as quickly as it had come, the feeling disappeared and he looked up at the barn, shrugged, and turned back the way he had come, walking along the edge of the water. And that allowed him, when he looked up, to see what he thought looked like a boat and a small pier about a hundred yards away. Had it been there before? He didn't think so, but then the last time he'd been back here, he'd mostly been worried about eight-legged wildlife. He walked toward the outhouse and from there he could see that it was, in fact, a boat, a long gray boat, and it didn't look to be in very good shape, but it had high sides and a big green outboard motor.

He walked up to the road and turned in the direction of the boat. The trees here grew thick in the narrow strip of land between the road and the marsh and he wondered how far he'd have to go and then suddenly he spotted a place where tire tracks ran down through the woods. The track led him through the scrubby pines to a small pier and there was the boat, chained to a post and secured with a padlock. A second chain and lock secured the engine to the boat, and he wondered if there were a lot of thieves around. How could that be? Heck, there weren't even any people around. There hadn't been a car over the road since he got up.

But it seemed like a weird place to keep a boat. Most of the time when you saw a boat tied to a dock there was a building nearby. Maybe they just did things differently out here. He shrugged, turned, and walked back out to the road. And then he heard a truck, a big truck, coming his way. He continued walking, getting almost to the house before the truck appeared over a low rise in the road. It was painted battleship gray, and as the truck went past he looked up at the heavy crane that rested on the bed and extended at least ten feet off the back. Right behind it came another even bigger truck hauling an empty flatbed trailer.

Clay made the connection quickly. They were coming to get the remains of the plane. He dashed into the house and shook his brother awake. "Aaron, wake up, they're getting ready to take the plane away!"

"Go away," Aaron said.

"Com'on, Aaron, I want to see them load it."

"What are you talking about?"

"The plane. They're going to take the plane away on a big truck."

"Go back to bed, will you?"

"Okay, you sleep your life away. I'm walking down to the beach to watch."

"Watch what?" Aaron did not wake up easily.

"The plane, you jerk! They're taking the plane away!"

Aaron's eyes popped open. "The plane? They're taking away the plane?"

"Jeesh, Aaron, that's what I said."

"Okay, okay, I'm awake." He threw back the light covers and dressed quickly and then walked outside and down to the outhouse while Clay waited for him on the porch.

"We gotta leave a note for Mom," Aaron said as he walked back up over the lawn.

"I already did, now com'on, I don't wanna miss this!"

"I'm hungry," Aaron said. "I'm gonna get some cereal."

Clay groaned. "Com'on, Aaron, breakfast can wait."

"Look, Clay, it won't happen as fast as you think. We'll eat a bowl of cereal and then we'll go, okay?"

"Oh, all right," Clay said.

Aaron got out the Cheerios and milk and sugar and they both ate quickly, even Aaron, who was finally awake. "Thanks for waking me up," he said between mouthfuls.

"I also found a boat," Clay said.

"Where?"

He pointed toward the road. "Down that way. It's got a motor on it and there's a road and a small dock."

"I don't remember seeing a house down there."

"There's just the dock and the boat."

"I wonder who owns it?"

Clay finished his cereal, picked up the bowl and tipped it to his mouth so he could drink down all the good sugary milk. "Com'on, let's go!"

Aaron drained the milk from his bowl and they headed out the door and onto the road, walking very quickly along.

The sun had climbed well above the horizon and already

it was hot, but it bothered them not at all as they walked through the fine morning air. More trucks passed them, smaller trucks and even a Jeep.

The pressure was too much and they began to jog along, picking up the pace until they were both running. When the road turned they could see the parking lot a half-mile away and they continued running because they could see the trucks and a lot of men in uniform walking around.

By the time they reached the lot, the crane truck had backed down toward the marsh and several men were dragging a heavy cable out through the shallow water to the charred remains of the plane.

The sweat they'd worked up in running dried quickly in the warm air and they stayed well out of the way, watching the men in the water wrap the cable around the fire-blackened fuselage. Finally, the man on the crane started the winch and slowly the plane swung around and started toward dry ground. Once there, the men changed the cable and the crane lifted the entire plane up onto the big flatbed trailer truck.

Meanwhile another group of men had been filling large barrels with the parts of the plane which had been piled in the parking lot. And then they made another sweep of the beach, walking ten abreast and maybe a foot apart, picking up even the tiniest pieces.

"They should've come at low tide," Aaron said. "I'll bet there's still a lot of stuff in the marsh and in the shallows."

"Wouldn't they have gotten that stuff yesterday?"

"Yeah, probably, but we'll need to watch where we step if we come over this way."

They heard a car and looked up, recognizing the maroon

Ford. They climbed down off the rock and walked over to the car as their mother climbed out.

"You two got up early," she said.

"It was really neat, Mom," Clay said. "They dragged it out of the marsh and then they put it onto the big truck. I didn't think that crane would be able to lift it."

"At least you ate some breakfast."

"Aaron wouldn't go till he ate," Clay said.

"We didn't miss anything, did we?"

"No ... but ..."

"I'm going up to the store to call the rest of the family. It just occurred to me that they might hear about it on the news and they'd have no way of knowing whether we were safe. You guys want to go?"

They both hopped into the car. The work was done here and a trip to the store might mean a new comic or candy. On the way they provided a detailed account of what they'd seen and they were almost there when Clay mentioned the boat.

"Do you think the man in the store would know who owns it?" Clay asked.

"What does it matter?" his mother asked.

"Well, maybe we could rent it," Clay said.

"What kind of a boat are we talking about here?"

"An outboard," Aaron said.

"I grew up sailing, remember?"

"But you will ask?"

"Okay," she said.

And while their mother called, they attacked the comic rack, checking carefully until they had each found one they wanted. Aaron went for a Classic Comic about Robin Hood and Clay went for a Scrooge McDuck. In the background they listened as their mother asked Mr. Watson about the boat.

"Oh, that belongs to George Bean. He had a rough time during the war, spent quite a bit of time in a hospital up in Boston and while he was there he got his law degree, but he doesn't practice. Lives by himself in a shack way back in the woods there, or so folks say. He gets a government check once a month and he spends most every day out fishing, even in the winter. Elsie Fisher over at the library tells me he takes out all sorts of books. Says she can't buy books fast enough for him. Reads everything."

"Is he, I mean, is he dangerous, Mr. Watson?" Linda asked.

"Who? George?" The idea took him by surprise. "No, not in the least. He grew up down in Orleans. Good family. Just wants to be by himself for a while, I'm guessing." Mr. Watson shook his head. "Terrible thing, a war. Some things just take a long time to get over. After I got back from France, it took me a couple of years before I began to put things out of my mind. George'll recover soon enough, I think. Some take longer than others. He was in the South Pacific. A pilot. He got shot down and spent a lot of time in the jungles." He shook his head. "Awful place from what I hear. But there's nothing to worry about. You'll see him coming and going on the high tide 'cause that's when it's easiest to get his boat through that little creek." He smiled. "He sure knows how to catch fish and if there's a clam to be found, it'll be George finds it. And you can't miss his truck. A black Chevy, pretty beat up, it is. Got a whole pile of fishing gear in the back.

You'll hear him before you see him. The muffler fell off last winter and he hasn't got around to replacing it yet."

"I didn't notice a driveway."

"Oh, it's there all right, but it's pretty well hidden. It's right on the curve before the beach. Doesn't look like much, just a hole in the woods. Goes a good ways back, quarter of a mile, anyway. Family owns the land, several hundred acres. Had it since forever." He shook his head again. "Awful thing, what a war does to a man. Used to be quite talkative, George was, before he went. Now, it's hard to get more than a couple of words out of him." He smiled. "He's also your landlord."

"I didn't know that," Linda said.

"He bought the place from his father."

And while their mother was busy talking they were taking in every word, even as they each picked up an additional comic, hoping they could slide it past. Aaron grinned. Mom was kind of down on comics. She said they didn't do anything to improve your mind, but heck, this was vacation and vacations were for letting your mind take a rest. And when they got home, they'd have only a few days before school started and it was well known that school was where you improved your mind.

"Hey, just a minute, you two," their mother said. "I see four comic books here."

"But, Mom, it's vacation!" Clay said.

And then, very much to their surprise, she gave in. "Oh, well, I don't suppose it'll hurt you all that much."

While she paid, they dashed out to the car.

"What's a landlord?" Clay asked.

"The man who owns the property."

"But not like a real lord."

"No. We don't have any of those here. Just in Europe."

"He sounds kind of spooky," Clay said.

"Clay, you think everything is spooky."

"No, I don't." He decided not to mention the barn.

"You do too."

"Yeah, prove it!"

"Hey, what does it matter?"

"I'm not afraid, you know."

Aaron decided not to say anything.

"Did you hear me? I said I'm not afraid."

"I know that," Aaron said.

"Oh."

"I also think you're right. He does sound kind of strange."

"What do you think he looks like?" Clay asked.

"Maybe we could spy on him, figure out when the tide's gonna be high and watch him from the woods."

"Yeah! Let's do that!"

"When we get back to the cottage, we'll check and see if the boat's there. If it's not then all we have to do is wait for the next high tide."

But now Clay had begun to think again about that strange feeling that had come over him out behind the house. It had almost been as if someone were calling his name in a very soft, whispery sort of voice. And he couldn't deny that it had pulled him toward the barn. On the other hand, more than once his imagination had led him astray, especially when it came to things under the bed. What he wondered now was what might be inside the barn.

4

George Bean

After supper, with their mother having settled into a book, they went outside and slipped off into the woods, working their way along through the underbrush until they came to a low rise from where they could watch. The tide had nearly reached the flood and now the little creek stood out plainly, twisting off through the marsh. They had nearly three hours before it got dark and they both began to wonder about their decision. It could be a long wait.

"We shoulda brought something to read," Aaron said.

"Or maybe some cards."

"Something, anyway."

They sat with their backs against a low-growing oak, both watching the road, waiting … waiting … waiting …

"This is pretty boring," Clay said.

"This is a whole lot more boring than that."

"It's worse than school."

"Nothing's worse than school."

"Well, waiting for the dentist is worse," Clay said. "You know what I wish? I wish we could go see the Red Sox play some time."

"Yeah, me too."

They both looked up as they heard the distant rumble of an engine, running without a muffler.

"He's coming," Clay said.

"Be quiet and keep low." Aaron pulled away from the tree and lay down on his stomach, finding a spot where he could look down toward the boat.

For Clay it was decision time. Lying down in the woods meant you were a lot closer to the spiders. If only he'd thought to bring a towel or something to lie on. But he hadn't and, in fact, he wouldn't have brought one if he'd thought of it because Aaron would have asked him why he was bringing a towel and then he'd have been in the same trap.

Aaron looked around at him. "Get down," he hissed. "Just like me! If you don't, he'll see you."

Slowly, Clay rolled onto his knees and finally, taking a very deep breath, he slid onto his stomach, expecting at any second to feel the searing stab of a spider bite, or at least he thought that's what it would feel like, because in truth he could only guess, never having been bitten by a spider. But nothing happened. He just lay there next to his brother, peering down at the boat and listening to the truck as it came down over the road in the woods, getting louder and louder.

At the corner the engine backfired and both boys jumped as if someone had unloaded a shotgun at them. And then they jumped again as the truck backfired a second time.

"What was that?" Clay whispered, his eyes wide, his mouth hanging open.

"A backfire, that's all. It's 'cause his truck doesn't have a muffler."

"I thought it was a gunshot." Clay laughed. "I thought I was gonna wet my pants."

Aaron laughed. "Just keep quiet. He's almost to the road."

They craned their necks up over the low underbrush and watched the battered old truck pull out onto the road and then turn in when it reached the track down to the pier. They had expected him to stop, but he drove right on into the woods, stopping when he got to the boat.

Both of them had tried to guess what George Bean might look like, but neither of them had expected the man who climbed out of the truck. In the first place he was very tall. His hair was black and long, and his chest was covered in thick curly hair. As he unloaded the truck the muscles in his back and arms rippled in the fading light and once, when he turned their way for a few seconds, they could see his bright blue eyes glinting from beneath heavy black eyebrows. He wore tan shorts and sneakers held together with white adhesive tape, and he moved very quickly.

He worked at a steady pace, lugging a can of gas for the motor, the oars, and then the anchor and several fishing rods and a bait bucket. Then he carried four big wooden boxes down from the truck and loaded them into the boat. On the last trip he carried a long stiff-looking case, and a gym bag.

He gassed up the motor, his arms stretched out holding the gas can over the back of the engine, and then he untied the boat and using an oar shoved it backward and turned the bow into the channel which was only a foot or so wider than the boat. Finally, he sat down, fiddled with the motor and then pulled the cord. It took a half dozen pulls before it kicked over and began to run, leaving a great cloud of bluish smoke behind as the boat started down the channel.

They watched the boat for a long, long way as it traced the sinuous, snakelike path through the grasses and then suddenly it disappeared and only the distant thumping of the motor remained and then that too faded away.

They both stood up and looked for the boat but they didn't see it again.

"Where did he go?" Clay asked.

"I don't know. He just disappeared."

"How could he do that?"

Aaron shrugged. "The grass must be higher out there."

"What were those marks on his legs?"

"Scars. Like on Uncle Nolan's legs. From the war." They had seen a lot of men with scars from the war.

"Well, at least now we know what he looks like."

"Yeah," Aaron said. And though he wasn't about to let on, one look at George Bean was all he wanted. In any of the movies he'd ever seen, he'd never seen a man who looked more like he was the bad guy.

"He's really tall," Clay said.

"He sure is," Aaron said.

"How tall would you guess?"

Aaron tried his best to estimate, but the tallest man he

knew was Mr. Johnson. He was six foot two and Mr. Bean looked a lot taller than that. "Maybe six-four."

"That is really tall, isn't it?"

"Yeah." He turned and headed back for the cottage, convinced he'd just seen the man who shot down the plane. He looked like the kind of guy who would do a thing like that.

Up ahead the oil lanterns shone from the cottage windows but they offered no help in getting through the woods. Both of them tripped and fell at least once and any number of times they caught themselves by grabbing a branch before they hit the ground. Finally, they stumbled out onto the scrub grass lawn and stopped.

"You okay?" Aaron asked.

"Yeah."

"I never tried to walk in the woods at night before."

"It was like a Tarzan movie."

"Were you scared?"

"Were you?" The one thing you never did, Clay thought, was admit weakness to your older brother. And then Aaron surprised him.

"I think so. I just wanted to get out of there. It felt like everything was closing in on me."

"That's why I wouldn't go into the underground fort you and Hank built. I knew when I looked in."

"So that's what that was all about. Afterward Hank said you were scared and I said that was a lot of crap because you were never scared of anything."

"You told Hank that?"

"Yeah."

"And you didn't even mention spiders?"

"You're not scared of spiders, Clay, you just don't like them. Like me with snakes when I was your age. Now, they don't matter so much. In fact, they're kind of neat."

They walked toward the house. "I don't think spiders are neat."

"But that's what I mean. As you get older you change." He opened the door, the spring at the top squealing. "We've got to fix that spring. It's a dead giveaway anytime we go out. Tomorrow I'll see if I can find an oil can in the barn."

"What else do you think we'll find in there?"

"I can tell you one thing we won't find."

"What's that?"

"George Bean."

They both tumbled on into the house, laughing about what it would be like if they threw open the door and found George Bean sitting there.

And yet, in the back of his mind, and not so very far back, Clay knew they would find something and he was pretty sure it wasn't going to be pleasant.

That night as they lay in bed, the only light coming from the half moon outside, Aaron thought more about George Bean, wondering what was in the long case he had seen him load into the boat. Was it a rifle? It looked big enough but he didn't know much about guns.

"Clay?"

"What?"

"Do you think he could have shot down that plane?"

"Why would you think that?" Clay asked.

"I don't know. But then I don't know why I thought he was scary looking. I mean we didn't get a really good look at him even, but I did think that."

"I didn't think he was scary looking, exactly."

"Maybe we need to get a better look at him," Aaron said.

"Sure, just go over there and introduce ourselves."

"Well, maybe not that ..."

Clay laughed. "What could he do?"

"I don't know. I just don't think it'd be a good idea, that's all."

"Well, maybe not. He is pretty big." Clay lay on his back, his hands tucked behind his head. "But I still don't think he looked all that mean."

"What we oughta do," Aaron said, "is get up on the next high tide and take another look. It'll be light enough then to get a better look."

"Who cares?"

"I do. I want to get a good look at him." He turned toward his brother. "I'm not gonna get close enough for him to catch me."

"Yeah, me either. That's why I'm not going."

"Maybe you're right."

"I know I'm right."

"But what if he did shoot the plane down? Isn't it our duty to find out and go to the police?"

"Duty? I don't know anything about duty, okay? I hate to say it, Aaron, but you get a lot of weird ideas, you know that? And I don't even agree with you. He isn't scary looking, but he doesn't look like the kind of man you mess around with either. I'm not going anywhere near George Bean."

"Okay, I can see that. I mean, like you said, he's big and he looks strong."

Clay rolled back toward his brother. "I suppose you thought Captain Bayles looked scary too, right?"

The idea took Aaron by surprise. "You thought Captain Bayles looked dangerous?"

"I didn't say that, you did."

"No, I didn't. But I need to get a closer look at George Bean."

Clay propped his head with his hand as he stared through the moonlit room. "Don't do it, Aaron. It's way too risky."

He heard the alarm in his brother's voice, but he knew he was gonna try. All he had to do was get out of bed in time for the next high tide, creep down, hide in the woods, and wait. But this time he planned to be a lot closer because the light would be weak then in the hour or so before dawn.

"Okay," Aaron said. "It was a bad idea anyway." Not often did he lie to his brother, in fact, he couldn't think of a time when he had. But he was lying now.

5

Spying On George Bean

Somehow he managed to wake in time. He checked the clock on the table between the beds, got up, put on long, dark pants and a dark blue sweatshirt, and slipped down the stairs, and remembering the squealing spring on the screen door, he opened the door only enough to let himself out, waiting for the spring to howl through the house, but nothing happened.

Instead of going through the woods and risking a lot of noise crunching through the brush, he took the road. Even in the dark the light gravel surface showed clearly and he trotted quickly along. He turned in on the path to the pier and when he reached the truck, slipped up into the woods and snuggled down into the low huckleberry bushes to wait.

The air was cool and damp coming in from the sea, but there was no wind and off in the distance he heard an owl hooting and then another owl answered from farther away. But those were the only sounds he heard. Slowly the sky in the east began to lighten and now, on the full tide, he could see the wide ribbon of water that led out through the marshes.

One thing was certain. Waiting like this was boring. He tried to think of other things, starting with chess. In his mind he played a series of moves with both the black and white pieces, concentrating hard to keep a picture of the entire board in his mind, as he had tried often enough before. But it took every bit of concentration he could summon, and after six moves by each player, he knew he had lost track of the board. He tried again and this time he got to seven and then, having shown improvement, he was about to try again when he picked up the faint sound of an outboard.

As he listened it came steadily closer and he pulled himself back into the huckleberry bushes and waited, the sound of the engine growing steadily louder and then, suddenly, it swept out from behind the cover of the grasses and he could make out a man standing in the boat, steering the motor with a long handle, as the bow of the boat threw a rolling white wave over the banks of the narrow creek.

As the boat came up toward the dock, George Bean bent over, shut down the motor and with an oar guided the boat gently up against the narrow, three-board-wide pier.

Once the boat had been tied, he began unloading, beginning with the big wooden boxes and then the rest of his gear. When he had finished, he stretched his arms over his head and then twisted from side to side to work the kinks out of his back. The light had grown much stronger and now instead of silhouettes, Aaron could make out details that minutes before had been blobs of dark objects.

The first thing he noticed was that the four boxes were full of lobsters and another was filled with some kind of fish. Finally, George Bean turned toward him and stepped out onto the pier. He worked steadily, without stopping, loading all but the box with the fish into the back of his truck.

Then, in the growing light, he knelt down on the pier and using a long, thin knife, he began filleting the fish. The big fish shown brightly silver in the dim light and his hands moved so fast that Aaron wondered how he could keep from cutting a finger. The remains of the fish went into a bucket and he laid the fillets on the pier, wet and shining in the light. He washed out the box that had held the fish and then washed each fillet and laid it in the box. The bucket of bones and guts went into a large barrel in the boat.

Then he used the bucket to wash off the pier. Finally, he picked up the fish box and carried both that and the bucket to the truck. He walked around to the door, climbed in, started the truck, turned on the lights, and drove out of the woods to the road. There he turned to the right and headed off toward the center of town.

Aaron pulled himself out of the brush and walked back to the road and then up to the cottage, trying to figure out just what he had seen that made him think George Bean was some sort of madman, because he sure didn't think that now. He shrugged. All he'd seen was a man who had gone out fishing and come back with a good catch of lobsters and fish and then worked at getting everything in order before taking his catch down to the market in Orleans ... or at least that was where he assumed he had gone.

He'd gotten a good look at the long case and he was pretty sure it held a gun of some kind and while that was ominous, he wondered if that was only because he didn't know much about guns and whether other fishermen took guns out with them. Why would they do that? Was it something that only George Bean did, or did he just not know enough about fishermen? He decided to hold off making a judgment about that until he knew more ... a lot more.

Nobody was up when he got back to the cottage and he slipped into the house and went to bed. But he didn't sleep. Instead, he lay there in the growing light, thinking about George Bean, and the more he thought, the stronger the feeling grew that there was something about him that seemed familiar, though he couldn't have said what, and certainly not who. But the thought did not easily go away. He tried to think of other things but just now that was impossible. His curiosity had begun to race forward and so far he had nothing much to satisfy that curiosity, and until he did he was not going to give up exploring. Maybe the next time he'd wait until George Bean had gone fishing and sneak up the road to his house and see what that looked like. You could tell a lot about someone by the kind of house they lived in. But that would be trespassing and you didn't go onto someone's property unless you had permission. You didn't even go cross lots unless you had permission, no matter how much time you could save.

The sun was up full when he heard his mother's voice calling up the stairs. "Com'on guys. Time to get up. Breakfast is nearly ready and we need to get an early start to do the shopping in Orleans."

They got out of bed and dressed and rumbled down the stairs and out to the outhouse, Clay, as always, holding back until he had no choice. By then Aaron was back inside washing up and Clay gritted his teeth, pulled open the door, and looked around. "Shoo," he said. "All spiders shoo!" He checked everywhere, and seeing nothing of any consequence, he finally he stepped inside and closed the door. As he sat down over the hole in the seat, his jaw began to ache from having his teeth so tightly clamped together. But there was no way he was gonna run! No way! No spider or any other kind of big ugly bug was gonna scare him away. No sir! This was just something he had to get used to.

He'd just finished buttoning his shorts when a soft scuffling sound under the floor of the outhouse stopped him as if he'd been turned to stone. What was that? He listened and hearing nothing more, stepped outside. He grinned to himself, picked up the bucket and carried it down to the water. Spiders were one thing, but wild animals he could deal with.

He lugged the bucket back and sloshed the water under the building at the back and a possum came humping out from under the outhouse, shook off the water and headed toward the woods.

See, he said to himself, you just have to take action, and now, feeling pretty pleased with himself, he walked up to the house. He could smell bacon and pancakes and there was nothing he liked better ... at least for breakfast. When it came to the other meals there were lots of things he liked.

"Hey, there," his mother called from the stove. "Wash

your hands and brush your teeth first."

He groaned and headed for the sink. At least the food hadn't hit the table yet so Aaron hadn't gotten ahead of him. He hated it when Aaron got his food first. It was a dumb thing to get upset about, he thought, but some things just didn't make much sense. He pumped the handle at the sink until the water ran into the pan beneath it and then brushed his teeth and washed his hands and face and dumped out the pan.

Linda set plates in front of them at the same time and Aaron, with his longer arms, got to the butter plate first and quickly slipped a slice of butter between each of his six pancakes and then handed the butter plate to Clay and picked up the syrup bottle.

Neither of them spoke, concentrating on the pancakes and bacon chased by swallows of cold milk.

"I thought we might look around a bit in Orleans," their mother said as she carried her plate and a cup of coffee to the table and sat down. "I know you guys aren't much for sight-seeing, but I thought it might be fun to do a little and I promise not to take too long."

"What kind of places?" Aaron asked.

Clay watched carefully, content to let Aaron stick his neck out and see what happened. It was the only good thing about having an older brother … well, maybe not the only good thing because, to be fair, Aaron was a lot better that his friends' older brothers. Those guys were mean.

"I'm not sure. It's not a very big place and I thought maybe we'd just take a drive around before we went to the market."

Aaron shrugged. "I guess so."

"You don't sound very happy about it."

"I'd rather be at the beach, that's all."

"We'll be back well before lunch and you guys never get to the beach before afternoon anyway."

"It's okay," Aaron said. "It might even be interesting."

Clay glanced at his brother and then quickly back down at his breakfast. What was he doing? Giving in? Why would he do that? The only time he did stuff like that was when he wanted something that was gonna be hard to get. One thing he knew for sure. Aaron hated to just ride around in the car almost as much as he did.

"How about you, Clay?" his mother asked. "Is that all right with you?"

"Uhh ... sure, I guess so."

She smiled. "Well, it's nice of you two guys to indulge your poor old mother once in a while and I promise not to take advantage of your kindness."

Clay smiled. "It's okay, Mom. I don't mind at all." It was a lie, a white lie, but sometimes you did that to help someone else. And at least now, he understood what Aaron had been up to, or at least he thought he did.

But he didn't get to ask until they had finished eating, cleaned up, and gone outside to wait for their mother.

"What was that all about?" Clay asked. "You hate riding in the car."

"What do you think?"

"You were being nice to Mom?"

"Think about it, Clay. We have each other to hang around with and talk to, but who does Mom have? I just thought it was fair that she should get to do something she wanted to. Maybe she'd even meet somebody she could talk to."

"Yeah, I can see that. I think you're right, but I can't believe you think about things like that. I never would have thought of that."

"You will as you get older."

"You think Mom's lonely?"

"Yeah."

"I never thought about that either."

"I didn't either until a while ago."

Clay shook his head. "I never thought about adults having the same feelings I have. That is pretty weird." He looked around at his brother. "What made you think of that?"

"It was after Mr. Crandell died and Mom said something about how lonely old Mrs. Crandell was. Remember how often she went over there to visit? And then Mrs. Crandell moved in with her daughter and it was okay again. That's what made me think of it. Adults need to have people their own age around just like we do."

"How long do you think we'll be gone?" Clay asked.

"We'll be home before lunch, just like she said."

He nodded. "Maybe we ought to let her take longer if she wants."

6

Worse Than Spiders

The strange thing, Aaron thought, was that while the tour of Orleans hadn't been very interesting, one thing had been close to astonishing. The Bean mansion. And indeed it was a mansion. The big, nearly square white house sat well back from the road, down a long driveway shaded by trees with little narrow leaves. A long, two-story wing ran out from the back and beyond it and off to one side a big gray shingled barn rose up into the trees. They would not have known who lived there but for a sign on the stone pillar on the right side of the iron gate which said, "Bean" in small gold letters.

Even then they would not have been sure that it was the same family, but in the checkout line at the A&P, their mother had asked about the house, and the woman behind the counter had made the connection for them. It was an old, old family, the woman had said and the house had been built by George Bean's great-grandfather, Captain Ebenezer Bean, who had himself sailed over the entire world. There was even a book about him, the woman said, and that made them a little later getting home, nothing would do but their mother had to stop at the library and take out the book. But that was Mom. She loved books and she wrote for a newspaper and she loved history. And once she got into a book she liked she always talked about it. Sometimes, Clay thought, that got pretty boring. He'd tried to read one of those books but it was pretty dull stuff. It was better to listen to his mother's explanation. But then, he wasn't much for reading unless he liked the story and it had plenty of action.

Mom talked all the way back to the cottage. "I can't wait to get started," she said. "Imagine sailing over the entire world." On and on she went, but at least it made the ride back seem pretty short.

Not until they'd unloaded the groceries and trooped outside, the screen door spring wailing at them like Bobby Parker's mother when somebody spilled something, did they remember the barn.

The building, roughly twenty feet wide and thirty feet long, sat off to the left of the house, the doors facing the road. It was set back far enough to allow a car to park in front of it and still allow the double doors to swing open. Like the cottage, the shingles had weathered a silvery gray and here and there shingles had fallen from the sides. The front doors looked as if they hadn't been opened in years. What they hadn't known until they walked around it was that the barn had a basement level with a door and two windows as well as windows in the back on the floor above.

Clay looked at the cobwebs draped across the windows and decided he had never seen a better place for spiders. It also looked as spooky as any place he'd ever seen. They walked around the far side and stopped at the front.

"I'll bet anything it's just full of neat stuff," Aaron said.

Clay did not mention the spiders. And now he kept waiting for the voice he was so sure he'd heard. But the only sound came from the wind, blowing steadily in from the sea, whistling softly in the eaves of the barn.

Aaron wrapped his hand around the handle on the right hand door and pulled it slowly open. The hinges creaked just the way the hinges creaked on the scariest radio show of all, *The Inner Sanctum*, and the sound sent chills up both their spines, rooting them to the ground outside, staring into the barn now lit by the open door and the windows in the back.

And indeed it was full of stuff; stuff packed right to the doors with only narrow walkways between.

"Wow," Aaron said. "Look at all the tools! I never saw so many tools!"

Clay looked up at the walls, hung with lines and buoys and lobster traps, and all kinds of rods and reels. "This is a treasure house!"

Aaron found the pull-chain catch and released the latch on the second door and swung that one open as well, flooding the building with light. "This is amazing," he said and he stepped into the closest walkway. "Look at this stuff! I never saw anything like this!"

Along the left wall there were axes and scythes, a long

crosscut saw, everything hung neatly and covered with cobwebs and rust as if it hadn't been disturbed in fifty years.
The rows, three of them, were bordered by lobster traps which
had been piled three high and three wide. Next to the traps
marker buoys hung from the walls, all of them the same, big
cork cylinders painted white with four wide vertical black
stripes meeting at the top.

Aaron stepped into the aisle and Clay followed closely.

"Do you think we should do this?" Clay asked

Aaron stopped and looked around at his brother. "It
wasn't locked," he said.

"I know but it isn't ours either."

"It comes with the house."

"How do you know that?"

Aaron shrugged, He didn't know that and he'd grown
up with rules about trespassing on other people's property,
even to cut through their yards you had to have permission,
but this was different, or at least he thought it was.

"Mom didn't say we couldn't go here," he said.

"Maybe she never thought of it."

He looked more carefully at his brother. "It's okay, I'm
sure it's okay."

"This is Mr. Bean's barn, isn't it?"

"I guess so. But we rented the cottage and if he didn't
want anyone to go into the barn he would have locked it."

"I suppose." Clay thought about George Bean and how
big he was and how powerful and how he moved so quickly.
"I wouldn't want to get Mr. Bean mad at me," he said.

Aaron grinned. "Yeah, me either. I never saw anybody
with muscles that big."

Clay backed out of the barn to stand on the sandy apron in front of the double doors. "This place is really spooky."

"No it isn't. It's just an old barn where somebody stored stuff. A fisherman." Aaron ran a hand across his spiky blond crew cut. "I don't think anybody's been in here in a long time. Look at the dust on everything."

"Maybe we oughta ask Mom," Clay said.

"Naw, it's okay. We'll just look around. As long as we don't touch anything it'll be okay." He walked down the aisle between the piled up lobster traps. "Com'on, Clay. We'll only look around, okay?"

Slowly Clay stepped back into the barn, his curiosity overcoming his reluctance as he walked down the aisle behind Aaron. But curious or not, he felt as if he had stepped into a forbidden place, and each time the wind whistled in the walls, he snapped his head around, expecting to see Mr. Bean coming after them. But there was nothing but the wind and he followed Aaron down to the back wall.

There, six windows looked out over the marsh and they could see the little creeks, running silver in the sunlight, tracing paths through the grasses. One of those creeks led right up to the back of the barn.

Below the windows a long work bench ran the whole way across the barn and the boards in the bench top showed the scars and wear of a place well used.

"Whoever lived here made his own traps." Aaron pointed to the bundles of red oak laths and the trap that sat on the bench half-completed.

"Why didn't he finish that one?" Clay asked.

"Weird, huh? Why would anyone just go off and leave it

that way?" He pointed to the bench. "He even left his tools on the bench. "It's like somebody called him to do something and he never came back."

"Weird." And then his eyes grew very wide and then even wider as the biggest spider he had ever seen crawled up from behind the bench and went waltzing slowly down the worn surface. He jumped back, wanting to run, but knowing if he did Aaron would never get off his case. So he pointed and tried to say something, but he couldn't make a sound. It was like the time he'd had laryngitis, except that now he couldn't even croak out a sound.

"Now, that is a big spider," Aaron said. He turned to look at Clay. "Hey, there's nothing to worry about."

The spider, a harmless wolf spider, stopped and turned toward them, waited several seconds and then hurried away, disappearing into the space between the bench and the wall.

"They b-b-bite, you know," Clay said.

"But not like a tarantula or a black widow. And they only bite to protect themselves or to capture what they eat."

"I know. I watched one tie up a fly," Clay said. "He wrapped him all up like a mummy." He shuddered. "Ugh, it makes my skin crawl to think of it."

"But they can't do that to a human. It'd take years for him to spin out that much web."

"But you gotta admit it's a scary thought."

Aaron laughed. "Okay, it's a scary thought. But nothing is going to stop me from exploring here. This place is incredible. And there are so many questions."

"Like what?" It was hard to think with the memory of that spider blocking up his mind. With its legs spread, it had been as big as his hand! And then he heard the sound again! Or he thought he had. He held his breath and this time he identified the sound. It was just the wind blowing through the cracks in the walls.

"Well, look at how neat everything is. See how the tools are hung on the walls and how he laid out the tools he was using on the bench? Look around. This was a place where someone built stuff. It's just the way Dad had his workshop laid out." He picked a draw shave from the bench, the blade still sharp despite the thin layer of rust. "This place is truly a treasure house."

"I thought you said we wouldn't touch anything."

Aaron set the draw shave back onto the bench. "Ooops. Forgot that. But I think it's okay. I mean, jeesh, Clay, how can I not touch things?"

"It's what you said."

"Okay, we just look."

Aaron walked slowly along, trying to look at each thing and everything at once and then he stopped and looked at the drawers that slid beneath the top of the bench. It was impossible. You had to touch things and in the matter of those drawers, he simply had to see what they held. He reached out and grabbed hold of the pull on the drawer front.

"Hey! You're touching that!" Clay said.

"I changed my mind about that," Aaron said. "I have to see what's in the drawers."

"Suppose there's ghosts in here and they don't want any-thing disturbed. Did you think about that?"

Aaron laughed. "You've been reading too many scary stories. There aren't any ghosts."

"Yeah? Says who?"

"Me, that's who."

"Well, how do you know so much?"

Aaron looked at his brother. "What are you so worried about? It's just an old barn filled with stuff."

"Maybe ..."

"What do you mean, maybe? That's what it is."

"Okay, okay ..."

Aaron opened the two drawers, looking down at the nails and screws stored carefully in separate jars by size.

Clay stepped in behind him, watching for another of those giant spiders. But his wariness faded when he got to the fishing gear, because if there was one thing Clay liked more than anything else it was fishing.

"Look at all the rods," he said. "Some of those are for deep sea fishing and they're all made of bamboo." Without giving it a thought, he reached up and spun the handle on one of the big Penn reels, listening to the spool click as it turned. "And they're in good shape too. I wonder if we could use them to fish with?"

"Where would we fish?"

"In the water, you jerk."

Aaron laughed. "I mean where would we get a boat?"

They both looked at each other and laughed.

"Probably not George Bean's boat, right?" Clay asked.

"That's even scarier than spiders."

"Com'on. Let's see what else is here."

Aaron stopped and looked down at the floor. "Hey, look, a trap door." He bent over, grabbed the metal ring set into the floor and pulled upward to reveal a set of stairs.

"Are you going down there?"

"It's just the cellar. There's nothing to worry about, Clay, cellars used to bother me too, but you get over stuff like that. I mean, when you think about it, what is there in a cellar that could possibly harm you? And beside there are windows. See how light it is?"

"Well there's …"

"What? Ghosts? Give it up, will you?"

"Well, there could be bats? Couldn't there be bats?"

"Sure. But they won't bother us."

But the truth was that whatever had spooked him, even when he'd been outside, had nothing to do with bats. He didn't know what it had to do with except that he was feeling scared and weird and he was even sweating the way he did when he had a nightmare. Step by step he followed his brother down the stairs, wondering if he would get over being afraid of everything.

"Hey, look, bikes!" Aaron walked over to where three bikes hung from the wall, two Schwinns and a Columbia. He reached up and squeezed the tire on the closest Schwinn. It was soft, but there was still some air in it. "I'll bet there's a pump around here somewhere. Man, if we could use the bikes we could ride up to the store anytime we wanted!"

"Do you think we can use them?"

"We can find out."

"Yeah," Clay said, "let's go find out. Who are you gonna ask? Mr. Bean?"

"Mom. We'll ask Mom and then she can ask Mr. Bean because he's our landlord."

"Okay, let's go."

"Man you are really jumpy, you know that? I want to look around first. What do you think is under that tarp?"

"It looks like a boat maybe."

Aaron grabbed one corner of the tarp and peeled it back. "That's exactly what it is." He pulled the canvas from the boat. "Wow! It looks like it's brand new!"

The boat, white with a red bottom, was about twenty feet long, and built in clinker fashion with each board overlapping the next from the gunwales to the keel.

Aaron knelt down on the dirt floor and looked up inside. "This is a really neat boat," he said

"How did it get in here?" Clay asked.

"What?"

"There's just the one door and there's no way anybody got a boat through there."

Aaron looked at the door and the boat, but it was clear that even if you set the boat on its side it wouldn't go through that door. It was barely wide enough to let a kid through.

"There has to be a way," Aaron said.

"But how?"

Aaron looked around. "There's a lot of room down here and ... look at that." He pointed to the floor and the two red oak rails that ran the length of the building from the stone foundation in front to the back wall where they disappeared. A wooden contraption sat, mounted on the rails and connected with a rope to a big pulley in the beam that rested on the stone foundation. Then he walked to the wood wall that faced the marsh and examined it more closely. "I think this whole wall opens up," he said. "See the hinges there? And I bet those rails go down to the water and the boat sat on that thing so it could slide down the rails and into the water."

Clay looked at the back wall and the big wheels hung from the ceiling above. "And I'll bet that's some kind of pulley system that he used to move the boat onto that carriage."

"It sure is," Aaron said. "Pretty neat, huh? All we'd have to do is turn the boat over, get it right side up and onto the carriage and then we run it to the water."

"Except that it's not our boat."

"I didn't say we wouldn't have to ask."

They spent several minutes exploring and then climbed the stairs and closed the trap door.

Clay decided he was getting used to this old building, but what really surprised him was when he discovered that he'd like to get a better look at the giant spider. He wondered if Aaron was right and that it wasn't dangerous. Aaron knew a lot of stuff about nature, but ... well, it would be foolish to take any chances, no matter what Aaron said.

He looked over at the bench and then up at the cobwebs on the ceiling. He wasn't sure what caught his eye, but something was out of place. He stared at it, trying to figure it out and then suddenly he shouted. "Hey, there's a trap door in the ceiling too."

"Where?"

"I think it's right there." He pointed to a small metal eye bolt. "And look, there's a wire from that ring." He traced it to the wall and down to where the wire had been wrapped around a two foot square concrete block.

"I wonder what's up there," Aaron said.

"You mean why did they wire it shut?"

"Exactly. The wire is to keep the door closed so it can't be

57

opened from the attic. Wouldn't it be more logical if the door was wired so nobody could get into the attic from here?"

"I don't think we should mess with this, Aaron."

"But to find out why they did it this way, we have to find out what's up there."

"Maybe we don't wanna know what's up there."

"What could it be?"

"I don't know, but ... but it's spooking me out again."

"Well, why don't you go outside and I'll find out."

"Alone? You'd go up there alone?"

"There's nothing to be scared of, Clay, com'on." He walked over to the bench and picked up a rusty wire cutter and tried to open it. "Do you see any oil around?"

"Oil? What do you want oil for?"

"Never mind," Aaron said. "I found some." He picked the old oil can with its bell-shaped bottom and long thin neck from a shelf on the wall and oiled the joint on the wire cutter. Then he moved the handles back and forth, working the oil into the joint until he could open and close the cutter easily.

He walked back to where the wire had been wrapped around the concrete block and snipped it free. Then he looked around, spotting a ladder about ten feet away and he carried it over, rested the ends against a beam, and climbed up. Aaron pushed against the trap door and the hinges squealed loudly as it rose up into the attic. He kept pushing until the door flopped back with a crash, producing a big cloud of dust.

He climbed down quickly and repositioned the ladder. And this time Clay felt the same pull he had felt in the yard only now it was stronger. He grabbed his brother's arm.

"Don't go up there," he said.

Aaron looked around at him, hearing the alarm in his voice. "Why not? It's just an old attic."

"No. Everything will change if we go up there."

"Jeeze, Clay, are you trying to scare me?"

"There's something up there," Clay said.

For the first time he hesitated, trying to decide if this was just another explosion of Clay's famous imagination. But what else could it be? There was no way he could know what was up there because he'd never been up there. Maybe it was one of those pre ... what were they called? Prem ... premonitions. Yeah, that was what they were called. But so what? "Clay, it's an attic and attics always have stuff in them. Now, com'on, let's take a look." He climbed back up with Clay right on his heels. The only thing in the room was an old rocking chair with its back toward them, angled so it faced the window that looked out over the marsh.

They walked toward the chair and when they got around it and looked, their mouths dropped and they ran for the ladder and then for the house.

The chair, having reacted to the uneven pressure on the floor boards as the boys ran off, began to rock very slowly, carrying the skeleton which sat there back and forth. The dress had faded with time, from the sunlight that came through the window, and a parchment-like skin still clung to the woman's bones. In her lap lay a long brass telescope, wrapped by the skeletal hands.

7

The Start Of Something

Linda had just run the last pieces of wash through the wringer on the washtub and dropped them into the basket ready to be hung on the line to dry, when the boys exploded into the kitchen both talking at once, their eyes wide with combination of horror and excitement.

"Slow down. I can't understand you. One at a time." She looked first at Aaron, simply because he was older. "Now what is this all about?"

"We found a skeleton in the barn," Aaron said. "It's wearing a dress and sitting in a rocking chair!"

"It even still has skin on it!" Clay added quickly.

"And she has a telescope!" Aaron shuddered. "I never saw a skeleton before."

"I guess I better go have a look."

Aaron was dumbfounded. "You want to look at it?"

"I think I better."

"I think you should call the police, Mom! Aren't you supposed to call the police when you find a dead person?"

"First I want to be sure this is not some figment of your imagination. So, let's go have a look."

Clay shook his head, unable to make up his mind. One part of him wanted to see it again because he was pretty sure he would never see another, and yet part of him was sure there would be a ghost nearby and he wasn't exactly eager about the possibility of finding out that ghosts were real. And there was no getting around the fact that he had known something was up there.

"Okay," Aaron said. "Let's go."

Clay brought up the rear, and he stayed back, the last to climb the ladder, feeling safe with his mother ahead of him, even as he craned his neck to the side to get a better look.

Aaron pointed to the chair. "She's there," he said and when his mother stepped past him both he and Clay followed, walking in a circle well away from the chair, staring at the remains of what must have been a small woman.

Linda stood looking down at the skeleton, thinking it must be a fake of some kind, a Halloween decoration that the owners had brought out each year. But clearly it was not. "I thought you were just making this up."

Clay and Aaron stared at the skeleton, taking in every single detail, even down to noticing that she hadn't been wearing shoes. This was a story that no one could top.

"Okay, I guess we'll go to the store and call the police.

But first I've got some wash to hang out." She turned toward the ladder and the boys raced ahead of her, each of them determined not to be caught up there alone with the skeleton even for a few seconds.

"Forget the wash, Mom," Aaron said. "We have to go right now!"

"No, the wash comes first. I'll not have my clean clothes getting all mildewed and have to wash them again. Besides, a few more minutes isn't going to matter much to that poor woman now."

"I wonder how long she's been sitting there?" Clay asked.

"I have no idea," their mother said.

"It looks like a mummy," Aaron said.

"There wasn't any smell," Clay said. "I thought dead bodies smelled."

"She's been there too long for there to be any odor left," their mother said.

They walked into the house and Aaron and Clay grabbed the handles on one basket and their mother picked up the second and they lugged the wash out to the clotheslines and began hanging it up.

"Do you think somebody killed her?" Aaron asked.

"I have no idea," their mother said.

"I didn't see any bullet holes," Clay said.

"Maybe she was poisoned."

"Maybe," their mother said, "there is a lot simpler explanation."

But they weren't interested in simple explanations and they plunged ahead, only quieting when they began to run out of violent possibilities.

Finally, just as they hung the last pieces of wash, Aaron said, "We should take some pictures or nobody at home will ever believe us."

"Good idea," Clay said and he ran for the house and the Kodak box camera.

"Now wait a minute," their mother said. "I think you should show some respect for the dead, don't you?"

"But, Mom," Aaron said. "We have to have at least a few pictures. We took pictures of the plane, didn't we?"

"But nobody died."

"Mom, please," Clay said. "We just have to."

"Well, I guess there's no harm, really."

They trooped back to the barn and up the ladder, and watched as their mother pointed the camera and took four pictures and then they climbed back down, put the camera in the house and drove up to the store.

Harvey Battersea, the constable, was the closest thing to a policeman they had in the town. He also owned the only garage and gas station in town and he had to get someone to cover for him, so they had been back at the cottage a half hour before he showed up, driving his old wrecker. He didn't say much at first, but then Harvey Battersea never said much at first. A lot depended on what there was to say but once wound up, Harvey could tell a tale with the best of story tellers. The one thing he wasn't used to was police work. They just never had any to speak of.

"Do you know who it might be?" Linda asked.

"Not for sure. Won't know even after I take a look. But I'm guessing it's old Mrs. Coleman. Went missing eight years ago. Searched everywhere." He looked around and smiled.

"Or so we thought. She lived there with her son Paul, who went off in his boat one morning and never come back. Pieces of the boat was found floating days later, but we never found the body. Happened in the summer, weather was calm, no storms, hardly any wind. Nobody ever figured out what busted up his boat.

"That was a year after Elvira went missing. Wonder no one ever thought to look in the loft of the barn." He shook his head. "Strange family. Kept to themselves. Two sons there were and both of them lost at sea. Father run off years before. Always thought there was a story there, but no one I knew ever heard it. The minister tried all right, but Elvira sent him packing." He shook his head again and this time clicked his tongue. "A fierce woman if ever there was one."

"Well," he said, "best to have a look."

The boys led the way into the barn, stopped at the ladder, and let the constable go first.

Harvey, who was short and sporting a pretty large belly, heaved himself up the ladder and the boys followed, their mother staying behind this time.

At the top of the ladder, Harvey hauled himself up onto the floor on his hands and knees and then slowly stood up and walked over to the rocker. "Yup," he said, "my guess is that's Elvira all right. Must've sat right here waiting for Paul to return from the sea. Had a telescope for watching 'n'everthing. Hard to say for sure, until the coroner has a look, but from the dress and the way her hair is all pulled off to one side, I'd say it was her." He stood looking at her for several seconds and then shook his head and sighed. "Well, at least that mystery is solved, not that it matters all that much anymore. No family from either side left. All gone. Nothing but a story for the newspaper. Be some puzzle trying to figure out how this happened."

He turned and headed for the ladder. "Would you boys mind going first and steadying the ladder for me?"

They scrambled down and held the ladder while Harvey came down a step at a time. He turned and smiled at them. "You folks have had a busy time since you got here. Most excitement in Eastham since Elvira disappeared. Suit me, it calmed down some. I got to go back up to the town hall and call the state police and the coroner. It'll take a couple of hours, so just keep the doors closed and go about your business. State police'll have some questions. I'll go tell George what happened, him being the owner of the property."

"We heard he had a bad time in the war," Linda said.

"That he did. But he was also the biggest hero to come from the Cape. Got all kinds of medals. Went to Harvard, afterward. Got himself a law degree. Smart as paint, he is."

Harvey climbed into the wrecker, backed out into the road and drove off, while they stood, watching the truck disappear, leaving a trail of road dust hanging in the air like fog.

"Well," their mother said, "I believe it's time for lunch and then a trip to the beach."

They dashed for the house at the summer speed, running as if the summer couldn't possibly last long enough to get everything done that needed doing.

8

Meeting George Bean

As soon as Mr. Battersea left, they packed the beach stu[ff] into the car and headed off. For a way the pines and oak[s] shaded the road on both sides, keeping the hot August su[n] at bay but after they passed the road to George Bean's pi[er] the trees on the left gave way to the broad open marsh. Whe[n] the road turned toward the beach, Aaron spotted the roa[d] that he thought must run up to George Bean's house.

Concealed by the scrub pines, the road appeared as litt[le] more than a vague hole in the trees and then they had gon[e] past it and now the marsh stretched nearly to the horizo[n] and the pitch smell from the pines floated strongly throug[h] the hot, moist air flowing in through the open windows [of] the car, mingling with the smell of the sea and an array [of] farm-like odors that rolled up from the marsh. But none of that got into the conversation. Now, all they could talk about was Elvira Coleman.

"What do you think happened to her sons?" Clay asked. "Did they drown?"

"What I think," Aaron said, "is there must have been a line squall somewhere out on the water that never got to shore. I read about them in a book. They just come up out of nowhere and disappear just as fast but they have really strong winds and lightning."

"Wow, I never heard of those before."

"And sometimes, when they're really fierce, they have waterspouts too."

"What's a waterspout?" Clay asked.

"It's a tornado at sea and they suck up a huge amount of water and when they stop all the water comes rushing down and it can easily crush a small boat."

"But if his boat got crushed at sea how come there's a boat in the barn?"

"He must have had two boats. Remember the other space? He must have kept the second boat there."

"Why would he have two boats?" Clay asked. "Why would anyone need two boats?"

"In case one had to be repaired. Sometimes boats begin to rot and boards need replacing."

That thought brought up another notion. "I didn't know that skin wouldn't rot away," Clay said. "It looked awful the way it was stretched over the skull and the hands."

"And did you see the way her hands were curled around the telescope?"

"Yeah, that was weird."

"And she had a pin on her dress. It looked like a seal, but it was so dusty it was hard to tell."

"And did you see her feet?" Clay asked.

"What about her feet?" their mother asked.

"The skin was stretched the same way. You can tell a lot about someone from their feet."

Aaron laughed, reached up from the back seat and pushed lightly against the back of his brother's head. "G'wan, you're making that up."

"Hey! No shoving. And anyway, I'm not making it up. Fat people have really wide feet and people who run things have a really long big toe."

"Where do you get this stuff, Clay?" Aaron laughed. "That is such a bunch of …"

"It is not! Betty Packard's Aunt Anne told us all about it. She even told us why girls paint their toenails."

Aaron waited. He knew he should shut up. He knew Clay was setting him up, but what the heck. You had to give your little brother a shot every now and then. "Okay, I'll bite," he said, "why do girls paint their toenails?"

Clay grinned. "Because feet are ugly."

Aaron groaned and then he laughed. "Maybe they ought to paint their ears too, 'cause ears are really ugly, like Mary Haley's ears. She should paint 'em red and get work as a stop light."

They both began to laugh.

"What about noses?" Clay asked.

"Easy there, old hoss," Aaron said, "or we'll have to go into the subject of people who only have one eyebrow."

"What's wrong with one eyebrow!"

"For one thing, you're the only one I know who has just one, except for chimps and gorillas."

"You're a jerk, you know that, Aaron?" He began to sulk and then he remembered Aaron's nose. "At least I can see from side to side with both eyes."

But Aaron was determined not to get drawn in. "Yeah, but I can smell things you can't. I can smell Billy Putman's dirty feet all the way across the classroom."

"Eeeuuu, that's awful."

"And that's not all I can smell. When the teachers come back from the lounge I can smell smoke on them. I can even tell whether they've been drinking tea or coffee. And some days I can tell what we're having for lunch."

"Can you really do that? I can't do any of that."

Linda, who had been quietly thinking about Elvira Coleman, suddenly began to pay attention. "Your nose is truly that good, Aaron?"

"Yeah. I don't always know what I'm smelling, but I can smell all kinds of things. Sometimes I have to go investigate. I could even smell the body but I didn't know what it was."

"I didn't smell anything," Linda said.

"Me either," Clay said. "What did it smell like?"

"A body," Aaron said and then laughed.

Clay laughed and so did Linda.

"But what did it really smell like?" Clay asked.

"Something old and musty, kind of like the way the woods smell after a rain." He stuck his nose up into the wind. "And right now I can smell dead fish."

Both his mother and brother tested the air.

"I don't smell anything but the marsh and the pines," his mother said.

"Me either," Clay said.

"I bet anything when we get to the beach we'll find a dead fish."

It was clear from their sidelong glances that neither of them believed him, but it didn't matter because he knew there was a dead fish on the beach.

And ten minutes later, down by the bluff, they found a big, rotting skate lying on the dried seaweed where it had floated in on the high tide during the night, and the odor was so strong they moved farther down the beach so they could get upwind.

As quickly as Aaron had gained an advantage, Clay brought him back to earth. "You're like a bloodhound, Aaron."

Being compared to a dog was not what he had in mind and the only thing to do was attack. "And that means I can track you down anytime, anyplace."

"No you can't."

"When we go back to the house I'll show you. I'll stay in the house and I won't peek and you go hide somewhere and I'll find you right away."

That was too much for Clay. "I'm going in the water." He pulled off his shirt and ran across the shallow sloping beach.

"Not too deep," their mother said.

"Jeez, Mom," Aaron said. "You'd have to go about a mile to find any deep water. And the tide's still going out." He tossed his shirt onto the blanket and ran after his brother.

"Hey, wait up!"

The water was wonderfully cool after the hot sun and they waded out until they were waist deep and then jumped and splashed and swam like two otters in the fine salty water. And when they tired of that, they walked back and forth, peering down through the clear water, looking for whatever they might find. But there was little on the sandy bottom beyond some snails and the tracks left by horseshoe crabs until they got to the edge toward one of the marshy islands. There the bottom grew muddier and Aaron could feel lumps beneath his feet, and Uncle Nolan had taught him the summer before at Giant's Neck, that meant quahogs.

"There's quahogs here," Aaron said. "I can feel them with my feet. Maybe we could get enough to make a chowder. He squatted down, digging into the bottom with his fingers. It took only seconds before he came up with a big, gray quahog. "See, I told you."

"How do you find them?"

"Feel around with your feet until you feel something hard under the sand and then go down and dig it out."

Clay suddenly looked skeptical. "What else is down there?"

"I don't know," Aaron said, "but there's nothing that's gonna hurt you." He squatted down and dug up another quahog. "We're gonna need something to carry this stuff in. See if Mom has something."

Clay looked in at the beach, which from here, seemed very far away. "You go. It's your idea."

"Com'on, Clay, just go see if she's got something." He dipped down and came up with another clam.

"No. I wanna find some clams too."

"Okay, then, find them."

"I'm standing on one now."

"Then dig it up." Aaron squatted down and pulled another quahog to the surface. Then he walked a short way off and set the four quahogs in a pile and while he was there he found two more. "I never saw so many clams. Wait'll Mom sees this." He looked at Clay, still standing where he had been, unwilling to move his foot and not ready to just go digging around in the mud and sand on the bottom. He might have forgotten about digging clams with Uncle Nolan but he hadn't forgotten the sea worms, big long ugly buggers with about a million legs, and they lived right there among the clams.

Here and there reed and grass-covered islands rose no more than a foot or two above the water, some of them running far out into the bay. They were close to one of those islands, which explained why they didn't hear the boat until it came around the end of the island and the engine stopped. And there was George Bean not twenty feet away, sitting on the back seat of his boat and smiling as the boat continued toward them.

Aaron stood dumbfounded, holding a quahog in each hand. But whatever it was he might have expected, it didn't occur. And there was something about the way Mr. Bean smiled that made you think you had known him a long time.

"You got anything to carry those quahogs in?" he asked.

"N-No," Aaron said.

Mr. Bean stood, picked up a long thick pole and poled his boat over to them. "I've got a basket here that should be just about right." He pulled a wire basket from the floor of his boat and handed it to Aaron. "Just put it in my boat when you're through." He smiled again. "By the way, I'm George Bean. I'm your landlord."

Aaron introduced himself and his brother, noticing that Clay's eyes looked as big as car headlights. "We wondered who owned the boat," he said.

"Kind of a beat up old scow, but it gets the job done." He ran a hand back over his long black hair. "I stopped by the other day to introduce myself, but no one was home."

"We go to the beach a lot."

"It's a great place," George said. "I've lived here most of my life and I never get tired of it."

"We heard you were a fisherman."

He nodded. "I do some fishing. In fact, I do a lot of fishing."

Clay moved closer. "What do you fish for?"

"Oh, mostly whatever's running. Right now, mostly blues and stripers, albacore, bonito. I also dig clams and quahogs and I have some lobster traps set out." He pointed to the two big wooden boxes in the boat. "Just finished checking my traps and stopped on the way in to dig clams until the tide came up enough to get my boat up the creek." He swept his hand through the air. "You fellas picked a good spot."

"I felt them under my feet," Aaron said.

"Good as any way I know to find quahogs."

And then it occurred to Aaron that if Mr. Bean had been out fishing, he might not know what had happened. "Have you been to the cottage today?" Aaron asked.

"I've been fishing for the past two nights."

"We went into the barn, I hope that was okay."

"Sure. It's part of the property you rented."

"Well, we explored everywhere and when we went upstairs we found Mrs. Coleman."

George Bean made no effort to hide his surprise. "Well, I'll be. Where?"

Clay shoved his way into the conversation. "In the attic of the barn. She was just a skeleton! And ... and she was sitting in a rocking chair holding a telescope! Then we went to the store and then Mr. Battersea came to the cottage and looked around and left and he said he was bringing back the state police and the coroner."

George Bean shook his head. "Well, that pretty much lays out the rest of my day for me. Guess I better get back and get cleaned up. I expect they'll want to talk to me, as the owner." He shook his head again. "Poor old woman, all her family gone and then she dies and nobody finds her for eight years."

"We never saw a skeleton before," Clay said.

"Me either," George said, "and I'm not sure I care to. Must have been quite a surprise."

Aaron laughed. "You bet it was. And it was ... well, I don't know what it was, other than scary."

"I wasn't scared a bit," Clay said.

"And I can see from the look on your face that probably not much scares you, young fella."

Aaron grinned, wondering how he had known that was a good thing to have said to Clay. More to his surprise, he discovered that he liked Mr. Bean. In fact, it was hard not to like him.

"Well, best I get started," Mr. Bean said. "I hate talking to officials, but some things you just have to do, I guess."

"The tide's still pretty low," Aaron said.

"It only means I'll have to pole part of the way when it gets too shallow to use the motor. One of these days I'll get old Bija Morton to come up here with his dredge and make me a channel so I can run in on any tide." He looked at them and smiled. "Well, dig a bunch of those quahogs."

"Thanks for the loan of the basket, Mr. Bean," Aaron said.

"No thanks necessary. And by the way, you can call me George, if you'd like."

They both nodded and watched him pole the boat quickly into deeper water before he started his outboard and went off on a diagonal line and then disappeared into the marsh. They could hear the outboard for a long time but the marsh grass was too high for them to see the boat. When they looked toward the beach they could see their mother standing up, shading her eyes from the sun, looking out at them.

"Clay, since you're not digging clams, you go tell Mom about George, okay? I want to dig some more so we can have a really good chowder."

"Okay," he said and off he went, eager to deliver his news, while Aaron went back to digging quahogs. And in what seemed like no time at all he had half-filled the basket and decided that was enough for a good big chowder.

By then it was time to get back to the cottage, in part because both Aaron and Clay wanted to be there when they carried Mrs. Coleman out and they wanted to see the state police and the coroner. Some stuff, you just didn't miss.

9

The Mystery Deepens

Well, it wasn't just one cop, it was half a dozen, and they were crawling all over the barn. They had to park on the road and as they climbed out of the car one of the cops came over to them.

"You can't park here," he said.

"I most certainly can," Linda said, "especially since you've taken up my entire driveway."

"Oh, I'm sorry. You must be Mrs. Harrison?"

"I am."

"Sorry about that, ma'am. I'm Sergeant Oberlin."

"It's nice to see you, Sergeant. These are my sons Aaron and Clay."

Sgt. Oberlin smiled. "You guys found the body?"

"Yes, sir," Aaron said. He'd never talked to a cop before and he wished he had his pants on instead of a wet bathing suit so he could stick his hands in his pockets.

Clay kept a half-step behind Aaron, content for once not to be in the lead.

"Can you tell me what happened?" Sgt. Oberlin asked.

"Clay spotted the trap door. When it's down you can't see it because the hinges are on the attic side and the cracks in the boards blend right in. A wire held it down, so we cut the wire and then we used the ladder to climb up. Do you think somebody trapped her up there?"

Sgt. Oberlin smiled. "No, I don't think so. I think there's something we don't understand yet, that's all. But the position of the ladder is important all right. Still, she was very old, in her eighties, so if she had decided to close the trap door and the ladder fell, she'd have had no way to get down. And from what Constable Battersea told me, they had no friends to check on them regularly. It could have been several months before anyone noticed that she wasn't around. No lights at night, that sort of thing." He shook his head. "But in those days, in the winter, it was even more deserted here than it is now." He smiled. "Thanks for your help," he said and then turned away and walked toward the barn.

"But what about the wire?" Clay asked.

Sgt. Oberlin stopped and looked back. "Right. You said the door was held by a wire."

"It ran down to the big concrete block."

"We'll check it out," Sgt. Oberlin said. He turned and walked back into the barn and they could hear him talking to someone inside but they couldn't make out what he said.

"I almost forgot about the wire," Clay said. "There's no way that could've been an accident."

"Somebody killed her and that's certain," Aaron said. "Now they just gotta figure who did it."

"Okay, you guys," their mother said, "go get out of your wet suits."

"But Mom, we want to watch," Clay said.

"How long will it take you to change?" she asked.

They ran for the house, talking as they ran, both of them jabbering at each other, unable to contain their excitement. It took them no more than a couple of minutes to swap their suits for their shorts and despite their eagerness to get back to the barn, they managed to hang their wet suits on the line, mostly because it was on the way, but also because they had been raised to help their mother.

They came up around the back of the house and they could see her talking to a tall, rangy man with black hair and very wide shoulders. He was dressed in carefully ironed white slacks and a blue shirt and he stood with his back to them, but they both knew who it was. Then their mother laughed and the easy natural quality of the sound she made, put them both at ease.

The man turned as they approached, smiling broadly. "How'd you guys make out with the quahogs?"

They both smiled. "We've got them in the sink ready to be opened."

"I'd be glad to help you with that," George Bean said.

"I wasn't sure how to get them open," Aaron said.

"I have to talk to the police and then maybe we can tackle the quahogs."

"That's awfully nice of you, Mr. Bean," Linda said.

"My pleasure," he said. "Nothing like good fresh clams for a chowder." He smiled at her. "And please. Call me George. I already told your sons that. I never liked being called Mr. Bean. Makes me feel like some kind of oversized vegetable."

Linda laughed. "All right, George it is," she said.

Clay jabbed Aaron with his elbow and whispered, "what's wrong with Mom?"

"You see it too?" Aaron asked.

"Yeah," Clay said. "She's acting pretty weird."

They followed George into the barn as he sought out the man in charge, who turned out not to be Sgt. Oberlin, but a short, round sort of man with a bald head, wearing a suit.

"H'lo Harry," George said. "I understand there's something of a mystery here."

"H'lo, George, how you been keepin'?"

They shook hands.

"Good as can be expected."

"Won't be certain till they check the dental records, but we're pretty sure it's Mrs. Coleman." He looked around at Aaron and Clay. "Pretty clever, these young fellas, to figure out there was a trap door there. Once you close it, it can't be seen a'tall." He smiled and shook his head. "Leave it to a couple of inquisitive boys, I always say."

"Any evidence of foul play?"

Harry, ran a hand over his bald head, looking down at the floor and then back up. "Can't say, just yet."

"Not likely you'll find any dental records. I don't think the Colemans were much for medical men."

"Judging by the state of her teeth, I'd say you're right. Most of them gone, the rest pretty well decayed and no sign of any fillings. Could be hard to identify her."

"How about broken bones?"

"Leg was broken once a long time ago."

"I'd ask Miss Myrna Longacre. She worked with a group at the church that helped folks out from time to time. I seem to remember a story about a woman with a broken leg that they made food for. Wouldn't go to the doctor. Her son put a splint on it and then just waited for it to heal. It could have been Mrs. Coleman, but Myrna would know for sure."

"Well, that's a help, by golly. It'd have taken me weeks of asking questions to find that out." He made some notes in a small notebook. "How's your father keeping?"

"Well enough. You know Dad. Doesn't want any help and can't do without it."

"How old is he now?"

"Eighty-seven. Perfect health, apart from arthritis."

"Tough as nails," Harry smiled and shook his head.

"That he is," George said.

Aaron and Clay drifted away from the conversation, poking around in the barn again, looking with greater care.

"Do you think her son trapped her there?" Clay asked.

"Who else?"

"But why would he do it?"

Aaron shrugged. "Maybe she wouldn't let him have any ice cream."

Clay laughed. "Or maybe she made him wear knickers."

"I remember reading in a book that sometimes people write stuff down," Aaron said.

"You mean like in a diary?"

"Yeah, a diary."

"But wouldn't somebody have found it?"

"Not if she'd hidden it really well. I mean, suppose she and her son didn't get along so she kept it hidden where he couldn't find it."

"Maybe they hated each other."

They thought that over, wondering if it were possible to truly hate your mother.

"I don't think so," Aaron said. "Even as mad as I get at Mom sometimes, I don't hate her. I could never hate her."

"But suppose she was really, really mean like the step-mother in Cinderella?"

"Maybe."

"I could hate anybody that mean," Clay said.

"Could anybody be that mean except in a story?"

"I never met anybody that mean, except maybe my fourth grade teacher, Mrs. Parsien. She was mean. No matter what the boys did they were wrong. She made us stand in the corner and she rapped our knuckles with a ruler."

"I think I spent most of the fourth grade standing in the corner," Aaron said.

"And none of the girls ever got punished for anything."

"I hope I don't get any more teachers like that."

Clay brightened. "But at least we thought of someone mean, like Mrs. Parsien, which means that Mrs. Coleman could have been like that too."

"I thought she looked pretty mean when we found her."

Clay looked startled and then catching his brother's expression he laughed. "Yeah," he said, "pretty mean."

"But it could be that he didn't intend to kill her. You know how old Mrs. Floggen wanders off and they have to keep looking for her? Suppose Mrs. Coleman did that and so when her son was going out fishing he put her up there and wired the trap door shut to keep her from wandering away. Maybe it was an accident. Maybe his boat sank and he got marooned on an island and by the time he got back she was dead."

"But why wouldn't he have told the police that instead of saying she was missing?"

Aaron nodded. "Good question. Maybe he thought the police would blame him for her death. Maybe he really meant to kill her."

"I think he meant to."

"Me too."

"Mrs. Floggen is pretty scary," Clay said. "I used to think she was a witch. Maybe Mrs. Coleman was a witch."

"What's that about witches?" George came up behind them.

"Just an old woman we know at home."

George nodded. "Let's go attack those quahogs."

They walked across the lawn to the house.

"You've got a lot of neat stuff in your barn," Clay said.

"You know, I've never really looked through it. I only looked in once. Most of it's too old to be of much use; all the ropes are pretty well rotted, and the beetles have gotten into the wood in the lobster traps. But I guess if I'd looked at it the right way, it would've looked like a treasure trove."

"Did you go downstairs?" Aaron asked.

"I never did." He laughed. "I guess that sounds pretty weird, doesn't it? I bought a piece of property and I never really checked it out."

"How much property do you own?" Aaron asked.

George grinned, hesitated, and then answered. "Quite a lot," he said. "I own this piece, of course and everything across the road and that land surrounds the piece my house is on. Several hundred acres."

"Wow," Clay said. "That is a lot."

"I've been buying land since I was in college." The squeaky spring howled as George pulled the door open, letting Aaron and Clay go through ahead of him.

Linda stood at the sink. "How's the investigation going?"

"I don't think we'll know what really happened," George said. He crossed to the sink and leaned against it, his arms folded across his chest. "It happened too long ago and there's just not much in the way of evidence."

"Do you think she was murdered?"

"Can't say. Sometimes what looks to be true is only a matter of not looking at things from another perspective."

She nodded and turned toward him, her position mimicking his own. "At the newspaper we see that all the time. The cops see things one way and then they gather their evidence with one conclusion in mind and ignore whatever else turns up. It's frustrating because all I can do is write my stories based upon the information they provide. I don't mean to say they're always wrong, but sometimes ... sometimes they go after a suspect as if it were a religious crusade."

"And that makes defense lawyers rich ... at least the good ones."

"What sort of lawyer did you plan to be?"

He chuckled. "Not that sort. I wanted to work with estates and real estate and businesses. I worked for a while with a firm in Boston but, well, some other things came up and I left and came home."

Adult conversations, Aaron decided, were too hard to follow. You could see from their faces that each of them understood what the other was saying, but instead of making things clear their words seemed to add more confusion.

"How did you get into the newspaper business?"

"At first it was something to do. I was a correspondent. But I like to write and English was my best subject in college and after a while they made me a full reporter."

"Where did you go to college?"

"Smith."

"Mom," Aaron butted in. "We need to get those quahogs opened."

"Okay," she said and then smiled at George. "But we have to make an agreement. If you're going to open all those clams, you have to stay to dinner." She smiled softly. "The real truth is, I have never made a chowder."

"Well, this promises to be fun," George said. He took off his shirt and hung it over the back of a chair and Aaron and Clay stood absolutely thunderstuck once again. His arms were huge and the muscles bulged from his shoulders. Then he reached into his back pocket and pulled out a knife neatly tucked into a leather sheath. "I couldn't remember whether there was a clam knife here so I took the liberty of bringing my own."

"I don't know what a clam knife looks like," Linda said.

Aaron looked around at his mother, wondering just what had gotten into her. He'd never seen her act like this, almost like one of the girls in school. He decided it must be from all the excitement.

"What else do you need?" Linda asked.

"A pot with a strainer."

"Coming up."

"Okay, guys," George said, "let me show you how to do this, so the next batch of clams you get, you'll know how." He picked up a big gray quahog. "The first thing we do is wash them clean so none of the sand and mud gets into the chowder. "Aaron, you run the pump handle and Clay, you rub each quahog in the water until all the grit is gone. Once we finish that we can begin the hard work."

Both boys set to work with a vengeance, and George also helped wash the quahogs. And, of course, some small amount of splashing occurred here and there accompanied by a good deal of laughter.

Finally, the last quahog had been washed and George took it in his hand. "See the way the clam is shaped? If you set it on the hinge of the shell it'll stand up and the place to open it is right at the top." He held it in his left hand and then he set the knife where the two halves of the shell came together and pressed the knife into the slot. "Once the blade goes in, you cut the two muscles which hold the shell closed." He pointed to two spots on the outside of the shell. "The muscles are about here and here." He worked the knife into the shell and ran it back and forth and then twisted the blade and the shell popped open. He cut the meat of the clam away from the shell and poured the juice and the meat into the strainer. "And that's all there is to it. I'll open some and you guys watch and then you can try."

He worked slowly so they could see what he did each time and after he'd opened a half dozen he stopped. "Okay, who wants to try first?"

"Me," Aaron said.

Their mother stood a little closer. "Is it safe?" she asked.

George stopped and looked down at the knife and then at the boys. "Have you guys used a knife before?"

They both shook their heads. Owning a knife was very high on *their* list for birthdays and Christmas, but very low on their mother's.

"Well, in that case we'll do this a little differently. Aaron, in the bottom drawer over there is a hammer, would you get that for me?"

He took the hammer from Aaron. "Now," George said, "I should've thought of this before. It takes a lot of pressure to open big quahogs and this is the safest way I know." He set a quahog on the sink board, placed the knife on the edge, and tapped it with the hammer, driving the knife down into the clam. Quickly, he picked up the clam so he lost as little juice as possible and held it over the strainer.

It looked a lot safer and now Clay's enthusiasm blossomed. "Do I get to try too?"

"Sure. Can't learn any other way."

Aaron balanced a clam on edge, placed the knife just as he'd been shown, tapped the hammer head against the back of the knife and nothing happened. He tapped it again and still the knife did not go down between the shell halves.

"Don't be afraid to use some power," George said.

Aaron hit it harder and this time the knife slipped into the clam. He held the clam over the strainer and very slowly worked the knife around, taking care to make sure it didn't slice into his hand, and suddenly the clam popped open.

"That's the way to do it, Aaron," George said.

"My turn," Clay said.

"Hey, let me do one more," Aaron shot back.

"Then I get to do two."

"Absolutely right," George said.

They spent the next half-hour opening the quahogs and when their hands grew tired, George took over and in what seemed like seconds he opened the rest of the clams.

"Now I've got a question for you guys. Have you ever done any fishing?"

"There's no place to fish at home," Clay said.

George looked over at Linda. "My boat's plenty big for all of us. There's flatfish running now, and the blues should return soon."

"It seems like a lot of trouble for you," Linda said.

"Not a bit. And I'll even take care of the lunch." He turned toward the boys. "Pretty strange about that wire on the trap door," he said.

"We figure somebody must've killed her," Clay said, "but Aaron said he thought that ..."

"Hey, no fair! That's my story."

"Sorry," Clay said.

"It could've been an accident," Aaron said, doing his best to sound grown-up. "Maybe she had taken to wandering off like Mrs. Floggen, so he kept her up there when he went out to fish. Then maybe he got stuck or maybe even marooned and couldn't get home. He would have gone to the police and told them but he might have been afraid the police would think he'd done it on purpose. So he told them she was missing."

"That's a pretty good theory," George said.

"And of course, old people wander off all the time, so all he had to do was tell them that she had taken to wandering and must have gotten lost," Linda said.

"I like this better all the time," George said. "I wonder if the police still have the records of their interviews with him."

"Did you know her son?" Aaron asked George.

"Paul. His name was Paul. No, I didn't know him. He was a lot older. I knew of him, though. Pretty surly. Quick temper. Got into his share of fights at the local tavern. He wasn't very big but he was strong. He pulled his nets and pots by hand and he was too cheap to buy an outboard so he rowed his boat. Work like that makes a man very strong. He got hauled before the judge, who was my uncle Roy ..." He stopped, watching the faces, and then looked up as Linda chuckled.

"You're kidding," she said. "Judge Roy Bean? The Law West of the Pecos? I don't believe it."

George grinned. "Well, he had the same name anyway, though so far as I know we aren't related."

"Who was Judge Roy Bean?" Clay asked.

"An old time judge out west. They also called him the hanging judge. But my Uncle Roy was not quite so harsh. He believed in settling things, especially when it came to a couple of men fighting. He said such things were bound to happen and he'd get them together in his chambers and talk it through and make them pay for any damages. After a while Paul Coleman gave up on fighting, in part because nobody wanted to fight him. He was, or so I've heard tell, as nasty as a badger in a fight."

Aaron nodded. It sounded to him like that was just the sort of man to kill someone ... even his own mother.

"We have a judge in our family too. Uncle Nolan. He's Mom's brother. He likes to fish and hunt and that's where Aaron learned to find quahogs."

George smiled. "Sounds like he's got his priorities straight."

Linda laughed. "You two ought to get along really well. I don't suppose you play chess. Nolan is mad about chess."

"Well, as a matter of fact, I used to play all the time. It's my favorite game."

When the cooking started, Aaron and Clay slipped on outside so they could see what the police were doing.

"He's pretty nice," Clay said.

"He sure is," Aaron said. "Did you see how fast he opened those clams?"

"I thought he was gonna be some mean and nasty guy from what the man in the store said."

"Yeah, me too. Boy would I like to have muscles like he's got. He must be as strong as an ox."

"I think Mom likes him," Clay said.

They looked at each other but said no more. The idea was simply too big and they both needed a lot of time to think it over. And anyway, they now had two mysteries to think about: Who had shot down the plane, and just how Mrs. Coleman had come to be in the attic with no way down?

10

The Black Queen

That night a thunderstorm broke right over them and Aaron lay in bed, watching the lightning and listening to the thunder and the rain hammering on the roof of the cottage. And then the wind picked up and for a while it sounded as if someone had turned a fire hose against the side of the building. He didn't know how long the storm lasted, but it seemed to go on a very long time and then with one last explosion of lightning and a clap of thunder that shook the cottage, the storm slipped by, leaving the night almost silent. Clay slept right through.

Aaron got up, opened the windows, and then climbed back into bed. He liked storms, even when the lightning came close, and he wondered if that was what it had been like on a battlefield. No. It must have been worse; in fact, he knew it had been worse, a lot worse because it had gone on for days at a time with bombs and artillery shells exploding as they hit the ground. What a terrible way to die, he thought, and much like what had happened to his father, except that he'd been on a sub that had been depth-charged. It hadn't sunk but they'd had to run on the surface and the Zeros had found them. He shivered, and slowly tears formed in the corners of his eyes as he tried to remember what his father had looked like and realized that all he could remember were the pictures of him at home. It wasn't fair, he thought, not fair at all, but then nothing much was.

He wiped the tears away with the back of his hand and tried to let his mind drift and slowly the normal night sounds returned, dominated by the chirping of the crickets, and he drifted off to sleep.

In the morning, early, Aaron and Clay began another exploration of the barn, but this time their search had a purpose. They were looking for a notebook or a diary or something written down. But after poring through every drawer in the work benches, looking through every cabinet and under every can and box, they had gained no ground.

"What seems strange," Aaron said, "is that there is nothing written anywhere. There aren't even any labels on anything. Didn't people used to do that?"

Clay shrugged. "So?"

"Well, it seems strange to me, that's all," Aaron said.

"I never write down anything once I'm not in school," Clay said.

Aaron laughed. "Yeah, me either. Except when I want to add something to the grocery list."

"I forgot about that." He grinned. "It isn't much use though. I write down potato chips every week and we never get any."

Aaron laughed. "Mom's really down on potato chips, all right."

"And soda. Don't forget soda. We never get any soda."

"But she makes cookies and cakes, and other desserts."

"Yeah, but it isn't the same."

"Were you still awake when George left?" Aaron asked.

"No."

"Me neither. I wonder how long he stayed."

Clay shrugged, then looked up suddenly. "Do you think the Colemans knew how to read and write?"

"I don't know."

"Let's check the boat and see if it has a name."

"What'll that prove? They could have had someone do it for them."

"But they were poor."

"Okay, let's check it out."

They scrambled downstairs to the basement, peeled back the tarp, and stood looking at the name on the back of the boat, neatly painted in white block letters: *The White Knight*.

"Strange name," Clay said.

"Weird. Why would you name a boat *The White Knight*?" He glanced to his left and then his right. "Look around and see if you can find a can of white paint and a brush small enough to paint letters."

They checked the shelves and almost immediately Clay

reached out and picked up a can of paint. "Here," he said. "Maybe this is it."

"Yeah, looks right."

It took a few minutes of searching before they came up with an old coffee can holding a round paintbrush. The brush had been left to dry out and the bristles were bent at the end where they had rested against the bottom of the can.

"What do you think?" Aaron asked.

"I think they could read and write and I think they painted the name on the boat."

"But why didn't they label things?"

"Because they knew where everything was. I've got all kinds of stuff I use to build my model planes and I never label any of it."

"But that works only if you use the same stuff all the time the way you do with your planes. If I didn't label things I wouldn't know what was where. You remember in Dad's shop how all the screws and nails are in jars with labels? That was 'cause he didn't use that stuff all the time and when he needed a certain size screw all he had to was read the label. It was to save time."

"But think of all the time you waste making things neat in the first place," Clay said.

It sounded like an accusation more than an observation. "What is this all about?"

"Aaron, you always have to have everything in its place. Look at your room at home."

"Is there something wrong with that?"

"I don't know any guys who pick up their rooms."

"This is a bunch of crap."

"Are you mad? What are you getting mad about?"

"Who said I was mad?"

Clay was loving every second. He'd gotten under his brother's skin and it was as if it gave him some power over him that he'd never had before. He was also smart enough to know to back off before it got out of hand because Aaron was not only bigger, but he was way too strong to mess with. Not that he was all that worried about getting into a fight, because Aaron had never once hit him, but sometimes, with bigger guys, you wanted to be on the safe side. "I didn't mean to make you mad," he said.

"I wasn't mad!"

"Okay, okay, jeesh, Aaron."

"I'm hungry, anyway." He walked to the stairs and climbed up out of sight.

Clay stayed where he was, his curiosity for now overriding his spider thoughts. There was something about this place that bothered him. He rubbed the top of his blond crewcut as he turned his head very slowly, trying not to miss a single detail. He walked along the walls, looking at the way the stones had been built up in stone wall fashion to make a foundation. In one place the stones seemed lighter in color than the rest, but he walked past, wondering just what he was looking for. He ended up back at the workbench holding the round-handled paintbrush, feeling the stiff and ruined bristles. The faint odor of turpentine rose in the air and he raised the brush to his nose to confirm where the smell had come from. Then he shrugged, put the brush back into the can, and walked to the stairs.

At the top, he closed the trap door and walked toward

the front of the barn and then stopped. Once again he was sure he had seen something that was either out of place, or was just odd. And this time he spotted it: four boards nailed together with cross slats to make a batten, leaning just inside the front wall. It looked like a door, but it was too narrow for a door. He walked closer and pulled it away from the wall and then as he looked at the side which had been hidden, he saw, painted across the front the words, *The Black Queen*. Wow! What was this? Then, up against the same wall, where they had been hidden by the first panel, he saw three more. One looked to be the same size, the others narrower. And when he stood them up he saw two more battens, both much smaller. He looked toward the door as he heard the sound of a vehicle slowing down, then leaned the boards back and stepped outside as George Bean's truck rolled into the driveway, the engine purring like a kitten.

"G'morning," George said as he stepped out.

"You fixed your truck," Clay said.

George nodded and looked back at the old rattletrap. "Yup, I did. Had that muffler around for months and this morning I decided it was time to stop terrorizing the tourists." He looked back around at Clay. "But I'll miss seeing 'em jump down in Orleans when it backfired."

Clay laughed, conjuring up the image of a bunch of tourists lugging beach gear, hearing the truck backfire and throwing everything in the air and running off the way people did in movies.

"Your Mom asked me to stop by for coffee," he said. "You had breakfast yet?"

"Nope."

"Good, then maybe I'm not too late." He stepped back to the truck, opened the door, and came back with a dozen eggs. He held up the box. "Fresh this morning."

"You've got chickens?"

"Yup. But no cow. Cows are too much trouble. Chickens, on the other hand, not only lay eggs, but if you let them roam they eat up the ticks."

They walked the short distance to the house.

"Chickens eat ticks?"

"They do. I've watched them. Anywhere else you go there are ticks, but where my chickens roam, there are no ticks a'tall. Makes my dog very happy."

"You've got a dog?"

"A big black lab named Captain Bean ... Captain Elijah Bean, the first sea captain in the family."

Clay opened the door and George followed him inside. "Good morning," he said, his voice warm and deep.

Aaron was already at the table and Linda stood at the gas stove, frying bacon. "Good morning," she said. "I didn't think you'd come."

"Invitation like that, I could hardly refuse."

Aaron looked at Clay and Clay rolled his eyes and then Aaron followed suit. Here we go again, Aaron thought. Another man around for a while and gone. But at least this one seemed to know stuff. The others, two from the church and one from her job at the newspaper, hadn't known anything. And he was pretty sure they didn't like kids. He sighed. Sometimes it seemed as if nobody liked kids.

George set the eggs on the counter and then he said something in a foreign language.

"Was that Latin?" Linda asked.

"The fruits of a classical education."

"And where did that occur?"

"At Bowdoin."

"In Maine."

He nodded.

"What did you say?"

"Beware of Greeks bearing gifts."

She laughed and both boys looked at each other and then back at their mother. Something had changed and it had showed first in the way she laughed. She sounded almost like a high school girl, like the way Babs Jenkins, their baby-sitter, sounded when she was talking on the phone.

George pitched right in without being asked and helped deliver the plates to the table and finally they all sat down and ate.

"Did you hear about the plane?" Clay asked.

"Only that it crashed and the pilot got out okay."

"We saw the whole thing," Aaron said.

"No kidding! That must have been exciting!" George said, but oddly he did not look as excited as he sounded.

"We think somebody shot it down," Clay said.

"Clay! We weren't supposed to tell anyone that!" Aaron said.

Clay looked down. "I forgot."

"It's okay," Linda said. "I don't think George is much of a security threat."

"They asked you not to say anything?" George asked.

Aaron nodded. "I think it had something to do with the investigation."

George's black eyebrows arched upward. "What made you think it was shot down?"

Clay looked at his mother and she nodded. "There was a bullet hole through the engine cowling."

"How do you know that?"

"We found the cowling," Aaron said, "and the pilot was there and he said it looked like a bullet hole to him."

"Well, that explains all the Coast Guard patrols. I wondered what was going on."

Suddenly Aaron began to worry. He had the feeling that something was wrong, but he couldn't for the life of him think what.

"Who would shoot down a plane?" Clay asked.

"Good question," George said. "A very good question." He shook his head. "It also took one heck of a pilot to land safely. It took someone with a really cool head under pressure."

"He said he was shot down once in the war," Clay said.

"In a war you're ready for anything," George said, "but when you don't expect something like that, when it takes you by surprise, then all bets are off."

"Mr. Battersea said you were in the war." Clay said.

"I was a pilot."

"Wow," Clay was always impressed with people who flew planes. He loved planes more than anything and the proof of that was the collection of finely crafted balsa wood models that hung from the ceiling of his room at home. "I'd like to be a pilot someday," he said.

George smiled and now as he listened to him, Aaron relaxed again. "I love flying," he said. "There's nothing like it.

I haven't been up in a plane since the war but recently I've been thinking of flying again." He frowned. "But maybe I won't do that after all."

No one asked why. They had learned that there were just some questions you didn't ask of men who had fought in the war. And Aaron thought there were plenty of other questions he'd like to ask, though he knew he would not ask them, at least not yet.

"George fixed his truck," Clay said.

"What brought that on?" Linda asked.

"Well, I'm not sure. Just seemed like it ought to be a little more presentable. It'll make my father happy, for one thing. He can't stand the noise when I stop in."

"Does he live in that really big house with the stone posts out front?"

"He does," George said.

"That's a huge house," Aaron said. "Does he live there all alone?"

"He has a woman who cooks and keeps house for him and makes sure he's all right. That's Mrs. Waters and there's no better person alive, I think. How she can put up with Dad and the way he grumbles about nearly everything, I have no idea."

"People like that qualify for sainthood," Linda said.

"Certain, they do," George said.

"I've never been inside a mansion," Clay said.

"Well, I'm not sure it's big enough to qualify as a mansion, but it is pretty big. Perhaps we can go visit Dad one of these days. He doesn't see enough young people any more."

11

George's House

Aaron stood looking at the battens stacked against th
wall, scratching his head as he tried to figure out what the
might have been intended for.

"Who is the Black Queen?" Clay asked.

"Who knows?" He looked round at his younger brothe
"I haven't got any idea. If I were home I could go to the l
brary or even maybe look it up in the encyclopedia."

"Maybe we should see if the boards fit together."

In the open space at the front of the barn they laid th
boards out. Clay saw immediately that the boards came i
pairs, and he and Aaron arranged them that way and the
stood, looking at them. Clay walked around and around an
suddenly he laughed. All the time spent putting planes t

gether had allowed him to see the final product in the pieces spread out on the floor.

"It's a box," he said. "Those pieces are the ends and those two make the sides and the others are the top and bottom." He looked back toward the workbench. "I need a hammer and some nails." He walked down the left row of lobster traps, picked up a hammer from the bench and then found a jar of six penny nails. "First we'll nail the ends to the bottom and then nail on the sides." He looked at the hammer. "Maybe you better put the nails in. I always bend 'em."

Aaron grinned at his brother. "Me? I can't even hit 'em!"

"Okay, I'll try, but I'm not used to driving nails."

"We need to change that," Aaron said.

Aaron held the boards together and Clay bent down, set the nail with a tap of the hammer, and then swung the hammer down against the nailhead. He missed cleanly and the hammer thunked against the wood. "See? I told you I'm no good at this."

"Keep trying."

On the second try he bent the nail, grumbled, and pulled it out with the claw on the hammer. But the third time he managed to hit the nail and drive it through the first board and into the one behind. "Hey! It worked."

Aaron lined up the boards and Clay drove a second nail, then went back and seated both nails, though not without missing cleanly a couple of times.

But now, with one end in place, they attacked the opposite end, and finally the side panels. Clay used only enough nails to hold the pieces in place and when they flipped it onto the bottom, the top fit perfectly.

"So, it's a box," Aaron said. "What's it for?"

Clay shrugged. "I haven't got that far yet."

"Pretty big box," Aaron said.

He nodded. "Pretty big box." He looked at the letters painted so neatly and evenly on the cover. They looked very much the same as the name on the stern of the boat downstairs and he assumed that they must have been painted by the same person.

"What would you use such a big box for?" Aaron asked. "You couldn't lift it once it was full."

"It would depend on how strong you were, wouldn't it?"

"But it would be hard to pick up because it's so long."

They heard the door close on the house and they could hear their mother and George talking as they crossed the yard. Aaron's first impulse was to stand up the box and hide the cover and then he decided to wait and see how George reacted to their discovery.

"What are you guys up to?" their mother asked. "We heard all sorts of hammering."

"We found these pieces of wood and put them together," Clay said. "At least we think that's how they go together."

George squatted down and looked at the box. "I can't see any other way for them to fit." He slid the cover back. "The battens were cut short inside to allow for the overlap."

"What on earth is the black queen?" Linda asked.

"I've got no idea," George said. "But it does sound familiar. Something from a long, long time ago. I'll ask my father. He's got a huge memory."

"It's kind of spooky," Clay said. "And there's a boat downstairs called *The White Knight*."

"It looks like the same person painted it," Aaron said.

"Let's go take a look," George said.

They trooped down the stairs and Aaron pulled off the tarp, and George looked at the name on the mahogany transom and then ran his hand over the bottom of the boat. "This is one heck of a boat," he said. "At least twenty-one, maybe twenty-two feet long, clinker-built, oak keel, cedar planking, mahogany transom ... one heck of a boat. Give me a hand and we'll turn it over."

The boys grabbed onto the bow and then watched in awe as George picked up the back end of the boat and rolled it to his left. He stopped when it lay on its gunwale. "Okay, let it down slowly and let it slide so it stays on the horses."

They did as he said, but it took all their strength to keep it from going too fast.

George began inspecting the boat, slowly, carefully, pushing his fingers against the wood here and there and then he took out his folding knife and poked the tip gently against the wood. "No rot anywhere. Whoever built this certainly knew what he was doing. There's at least four coats of varnish on the inside. I don't think it's ever been in the water." He examined the seams on the stern where the side planks had been joined to the mahogany transom.

"There's even a track to get it into the water." Aaron pointed to the carriage that rode on the oak rails.

George smiled and then looked up to the ceiling. "And there's a hoist too. All we have to do is put the slings under it and then swing it over to the carriage and let it down." He pointed to the far wall where another block and fall hung from the sill beam. "There's another tackle there so you can move the boat through the air and get it into position by pulling on one and releasing the other."

"Are you gonna put it in the water?" Clay asked.

"Yup," George said. "It'll leak some at first, but it should swell up quickly enough. I don't think the leaks will amount to much the way this boat was built. I was gonna buy a new motor for my boat this week, but now I think I'll put it on this one. She's built to take heavy water. See the way the bow rises and curves to the outside? She'll take a lot of sea."

"You ought to change the name, though," Linda said.

"Why?" George asked.

"It just doesn't seem like a boat name."

George laughed. "First let's see if she'll float. We'll get her ready and then slide her down the ways."

"The ways?" Aaron asked.

"Those rails in the floor are called ways. They use much the same thing in boatyards. Even ships are launched that way." He lowered the big block and fall and then checked the ropes to make sure they were sound. They weren't and he pulled one of them apart easily. "Well, guess I'll have to get some rope from the house."

"Today?" Clay asked.

"Sure. Why don't we all go and then you can meet my dog and see where I live."

They rode up in the car, bouncing over the potholes and ruts in the dirt road that wound back up into the woods, the trees growing larger as they moved up away from the shore, and finally they came around a turn in the road and there was the house. It looked like no house any of them had seen before. Covered in silvery gray shingles, it seemed to head in different directions almost as if whoever built it had suddenly tired of going one way and decided to build a wing off in another direction. The four wings were built from a central octagon which rose up three stories to a tower with windows on all sides. It even had a deck the whole way around.

As they pulled up into the circular drive, Aaron glanced at the big barn to his right and then quickly back as a very big black Lab bounced down from the front porch and barked them to a stop.

"That, as you can see, is Captain."

"Is he okay?" Clay asked.

"Captain?" The question had clearly surprised him. "Best dog there ever was." He climbed out of the car and reached down, scratching around the dog's ears. "Got some visitors, old boy, and you don't get many of those."

They got out of the car and immediately Captain came up to them, sniffing and panting, and Linda reached out and ran a hand along his cheek and made a friend for life. Still, even after Aaron began petting the dog, Clay held back. Having been bitten by an Airedale, he put great store in the old saying, "once bitten, twice cautious."

But Captain wasn't having any of that and he rubbed up against Clay and lifted his head.

Clay smiled. "I think he likes me."

"Of course he does," George said. "Old Captain'll soak up all the petting he can get."

Clay reached down and brushed the soft black fur on Captain's broad head as he looked into the gentle yellow eyes.

"I heard you lived in a shack," Linda said.

George grinned. "There are a lot of rumors about me. I live alone and I keep to myself and because the family is well-known, people talk about us. Rumors. In the winter, once the tourists are gone, everybody talks about everybody else. Ten months of the year we're a collection of very small towns well removed from the outside world."

Aaron and Clay walked on ahead moving fast enough to get out of range and Captain bounded along with them.

"I wish we had a dog," Aaron said.

"It sure is a big house. Not even the tobacco farmers at home have houses any bigger."

Aaron looked off to his right toward the barn. "Hey, let's go look at the chickens."

They ran that way and Captain stayed right with them, trotting along and finally breaking into a lope. And like any bird dog, he was very interested in the chickens. Mostly he wanted to get them outside in the open where he could run them down, and while Aaron and Clay stood watching the hens scratching and clucking inside the big pen, Captain circled the wire, looking for a way in and the big rooster stayed with him, his tail up, his head back, ready to attack.

'That is a really nasty looking rooster," Aaron said.

"Look at those pointed things on the inside of his legs." Clay shook his head. "I never knew roosters had those."

"Hey," their mother called, "come see the house."

They turned away from the chickens and Clay set the pace. "Com'on, Aaron, faster," he said.

"You go ahead," Aaron said.

"Are you okay?"

"Sure."

"You've been acting funny."

Aaron shrugged. "It's okay. I didn't sleep well last night."

"Yeah, me either. I kept seeing the skeleton." He shivered. "Her face with the dried skin really spooked me."

Aaron chuckled. "Me too," he said, deliberately letting Clay think that's what was bothering him. It was too soon to say anything anyway, but he knew it was coming. Sooner or later Mom would meet another man and get married, and … and … that was gonna change everything. The hard part was knowing for sure whether it would be for the good. The other men who had come to dinner hadn't lasted long. George was different. He even seemed to like kids, but that was something you had to watch. Billy Brown's stepfather seemed to like kids too and then, afterward, there was all kinds of trouble and one time the police had to come. And anyway, he didn't need a stepfather. They were doing fine.

George led them through the house and Aaron had to admit it was like nothing he'd ever seen before. The rooms were all large and it had four bedrooms, each with its own bathroom but the best part was the tower. You could see out over the water for miles and miles and miles and the piece of land was so high that you could even see back across the Cape to the Atlantic Ocean.

"I spend a lot of time up here," George said. "From here I can watch the sun rise and see it set. I can identify ships at sea and I can watch the weather come in from a long way off. It gives me some perspective."

"Is that land I see in the distance?" Clay asked.

"That's the other side of Cape Cod Bay."

The conversation drifted one way and another and Aaron

shut it out, thinking now about the boat back in the barn and trying to recall every detail of what he had seen. And then as he looked out at the old target hulk sitting on the reef, he remembered the plane.

"How close would you have to be to shoot down a plane that way?" he asked.

"Pretty close," George said. "And you'd have to be an awfully good shot to hit something moving that fast."

"What kind of a gun would you use?"

"An M-1 would do it, I think. How big was the hole?"

"Fifty caliber. That's right, isn't it, Mom?" Aaron asked.

"It is." She looked around at George.

George shook his head. "The only fifty calibers I know of are elephant guns." He shook his head. "But they wouldn't have enough range." He grinned. "Do you guys always turn up mysteries like this?"

"Mostly," Clay said, "things are pretty boring."

"Yeah," Aaron said, "same old stuff all the time."

"Well, I like that," Linda said. "You make us sound like a family that never does anything."

"We never go to Fenway Park," Aaron said.

"We need to do that, Mom," Clay said. "We need to go to Fenway and see Ted Williams play. How can a guy learn to hit a baseball unless he gets to see Ted Williams?"

George grinned but said nothing.

"I didn't even know you wanted to go," Linda said. "We'll talk about this later, okay?"

"Can we go?" Aaron asked.

"I didn't say that. I said we'll talk about it."

Aaron knew what that meant. No Fenway. Whenever his

mother said "we'll talk about it" it meant she was going to tell them why whatever it was they wanted wasn't going to happen. She'd done that a lot with the dog issue and they still didn't have a dog. It hadn't helped at all when Clay got bitten by that stupid Airedale.

"Let's go get that rope," George said. "I'd like to get the boat into the water and see how much it leaks."

As they walked through the living room, Aaron spotted a big chess set sitting on a marble board. It looked as if someone had stopped in the middle of a game and he hung back because he had never seen a set like this one. The pieces looked as if they were made of some kind of stone and he stood with his hands in his pockets, looking down at them, wanting very badly just to pick one up, but knowing that he could not unless he asked.

"Do you play chess?" George walked over to the table.

"I'm just learning," Aaron said. "This is a beautiful set."

"I bought it from an antique dealer in Boston," George said. "It's all marble."

"The pieces are really big. Can I pick one up?"

"Sure. Just put it back in the same place. I haven't finished the game."

"Who do you play with?"

"No one at the moment. I was just working out my own version of a knight's gambit." He chuckled. "I captured the queen, as you can see, but at the cost of my knight. What I'm trying to do is capture the queen without losing the knight. Maybe we could play a game sometime."

"I'm not very good," Aaron said.

"Well, that means you can only get better, right?"

Aaron grinned. "I hadn't thought of it that way."

"Wow ..." Clay said. "I never saw so many guns!"

They all turned toward him as he stood in front of a very long glass-fronted case built into the north wall.

"What do you use them for?" Clay asked.

"Mostly for hunting. That's what Captain does. He hunts and retrieves. I only had a couple of rifles and shotguns and then when Dad couldn't hunt anymore he gave me his guns. He's hunted all over the world. He's got one room that's just filled with trophies; a lion, a tiger, a leopard, all sorts of antelope, a grizzly. I was too young to go with him on those trips and then the war came just when I got old enough." He shook his head and smiled. "But I get all the hunting I want here, pheasants, ducks, deer, quail. All I want."

"Which kind of guns are which?" Aaron asked.

George took a key ring from his pocket and opened one of the doors. "These are all shotguns. The twelve gauge guns are for ducks and I use the twenty gauge guns for everything else. For deer I use a rifle." He grinned. "The truth is, if you look closely, you can see three guns which look pretty well used. Those are mine. I use Dad's now and then, but he bought all those guns in England and I just can't bring myself to sit in a duck blind holding a shotgun that cost what for most people is a year's pay. I just keep them oiled and shoot some clay pigeons now and then. Dad hunted with all of them at different times. He's shot about every big game animal in the world, including rhino and elephant."

"He must be really rich," Clay said.

George smiled. "He was gone a lot. Some years it seemed like he was never home. My mother died when I was born."

"How awful," Linda said.

"I suppose it was, but then I never knew anything else. I was raised by a nanny, a wonderful woman, Mary O'Neill. She died when I was in the Pacific." Suddenly he looked around at them and smiled. "This is getting a little too gloomy. Let's get the rope and get that boat into the water." He looked at his watch. "I'm going to Orleans to pick up a motor."

Aaron and George gathered the rope, a single coil of three-quarter-inch hemp, and loaded it into the trunk, while Clay sat outside petting Captain and talking to his mother. Then they drove back to the cottage, leaving Captain sitting on the porch, watching them leave.

"Doesn't Captain run away?" Clay asked

"Nope. He just takes care of the place till I get back. He stays out most of the year, sleeping on the porch. In the winter, when it gets really cold he comes inside, but he prefers to be out. He has a shelter on the porch where he can get out of the wind. When he gets older he'll want to come inside more."

"He's a really nice dog," Clay said.

"Best dog I ever had," George said. "I'm getting him a girlfriend from a breeder in Orleans later in the month. Nothing like having a puppy around." He looked around at Linda. "Would you like to see the pups?"

"Sure," Aaron said. "Are they for sale?"

"I think they're all spoken for."

"But it would be fun to see them," Clay said. "I've never seen a whole bunch of puppies at once."

"It would be nice to see them," Linda said, and Aaron could tell from the tone of her voice that she was not enthusiastic about the subject having come up again.

12

Water Power

It was fun, just plain fun. They had opened the doors completely and now the room, flooded with light and air, had surrendered the dank musty feeling to the outside air.

And whatever their misgivings about George, he made the work interesting, explaining everything he did, and showing them how to help. First, he replaced the ropes in the overhead hoist, then made a sling under the boat which he hooked to the hoist. That done, he climbed a ladder and oiled the block and fall attached to the supporting timbers of the barn and repeated the procedure with the tackle on the far wall. Then he slung another rope around the boat and hooked it to the ropes from the pulley on the far wall. Finally, he got a bucket of water from the creek, and soaked the two oak rails.

"Okay, Aaron, you and Clay take hold of the rope that comes out of the pulley over there." He pointed toward the wall. "I'll haul on this one and once the boat is high enough, you guys pull and draw the boat toward the cradle and I'll let off line slowly so the boat moves over to the cradle." He turned. "Linda, your job is to stay at the bow and make sure the boat doesn't swing to one side or the other so we can lower it straight down onto the cradle."

George pulled on the rope and slowly the boat came up off the horses and rose to a couple of feet above them. "Okay, guys, start hauling on that rope."

Aaron and Clay did just as they'd been told, and with George guiding the side and Linda the bow, the boat moved through the air until it was directly above the cradle. "Now slack off on your line," George said, and slowly the boat settled down into the cradle.

"Perfect," George said. "Nobody could have done that any better, guys."

"That boat is really heavy," Aaron said.

"That's because it's well built," George said. He ran his hand along the gunwale. "Whoever built this knew what he was doing. All the lines are true." He shook his head and clicked his tongue softly. "The funny thing is how familiar it looks, and yet I'm pretty sure I've never seen a boat just like it. Years ago there was a boat builder down in Orleans who built the finest wood boats on the Cape. Mostly he built what we call cat boats. I'll have to ask Homer Dodge, he'll remember." He bent over and picked up another coil of rope and pulled the end loose. "Here comes the test," he said. "You guys watched me rig that block and fall, right? Well, let's see if you can rig this rope into the tackle on the back wall. It looks different, but it comes down to the same thing. Meantime, I'll wade out and run this end of the line through the pulley on that post in the marsh."

Aaron picked up the loose end of the rope and pulled it back to the big pulley wheels attached to the sill on the front wall of the barn. It had looked easy enough and there had been no doubt in their minds that they could do it, but suddenly they were stumped.

"Bring the rope over to the back pulley," Clay said.

Aaron grinned. "And then through the front and then to the back and finally to the front?"

Clay smiled. "I think so but it's kind of confusing."

They led the rope through the first block. "How much do we pull through?" Clay asked.

Aaron shrugged. "I don't know. Enough so we can pull on it, I think."

"Yeah. Sounds right."

They fed some ten feet of rope through and then wove the rope back and forth through the pulley blocks. It looked right, but they'd never done anything like this before.

"Did you get it?" their mother asked.

"Sure," Aaron said. "Nothing to it."

George came back with a full bucket of water and set it by the door where they could wet the rails again as the cradle moved along the ways, and then they hauled on the long rope and the big boat slid slowly down into the water, the cradle submerging until the boat floated free but still tied to the cradle so it stayed in place. George had left enough slack so the boat could float up on the tide.

"Now let's see if it leaks," George said.

They all walked down and looked into the boat. Not a drop of water showed.

"So far so good," George said, "but we'll give it a while for the water to find its way in. Sometimes, a clinker-built boat like this, because of the way one board overlaps another, will stay sound." He grinned. "But it isn't likely."

"If it leaks," Clay asked, "how long will it take before it doesn't?"

George smiled. "Hard to say for sure. In a couple of days it'll probably swell up enough. The boat's been out of water for some time, but it was stored inside and the dirt floor in the barn is pretty damp, so the wood may not have shrunk too badly."

"Why didn't it rot?" Aaron asked.

"You guys ask good questions. Two answers. One, the wood is cedar and cedar lasts a long time. What's more this boat had been well cared for. The bottom is covered with red lead paint and there's no sign of peeling on the sides. The inside has been varnished and it was done right."

"Are we going to leave the cradle under it?" Clay asked.

"We are," George said. "Can you think why?"

"So if it sinks, we'll have a way to get it back out for repairs," Aaron said.

"Smart guys, you two are, all right," George said. "Smart as paint, as the fella says."

Linda smiled at her sons. "You guys did that really well," she said. "And now I think it's lunchtime." She turned to George. "Will you eat with us?"

He smiled. "No, but thank you. I've got to get down to

Orleans to see about that motor and then visit my father."
He smiled at the boys. "You know if you guys hadn't gone
poking round in the barn, I probably would never have
looked. And now I discover I'm the owner of a first-rate boat."
He looked back at the boat, turned, and started for his truck.
"Thanks for all your help getting it into the water. You guys
did a heck of a job. Did everything just right. And once I get
a motor on it, we'll go fishing, if your mother says it's okay."

Aaron looked at his mother and there was that look again,
a look he had never seen before yesterday and now was turning up all the time, and it was making him pretty nervous.

After lunch they spent more time scouring the barn and
checking on the boat which now had some water at the very
bottom by the keel, but only an inch or so, and it didn't seem
to be getting any deeper.

"Hey guys!" their mother called from the back porch.
"Beach time! Your suits are on the line."

In minutes they had put on their suits, grabbed their towels, and headed for the car.

"I'm in front!" Clay called.

"No you're not!" Aaron shouted back over his shoulder.
"It's my turn!"

"Says who?"

"Says me!" He opened the door and climbed in, then
closed the door before Clay reached the car.

"Com'on, Aaron! This isn't fair. It's my turn. You rode
shotgun yesterday!"

His mother opened the driver's side door. "Aaron, you
did ride shotgun yesterday."

"I did not!"

"Aaron, you most certainly did."

"Who made you king of the world?"

"Aaron!"

"What? What did I do now?"

"Perhaps you'd prefer to stay in your room while we go to the beach."

"I get sick in the back seat."

"Nice try," his mother said. "We're only going a mile, if that."

"I should get to ride here all the time because I'm older."

"Aaron? What is going on here? You know you rode shotgun last and you've never pulled a stunt like this before. You've been a really good big brother to Clay, always willing to share ... so what's going on here?"

"Today is different, that's all."

"No. It's just the same ... maybe a little hotter, and I'm getting very hot just now and I want to get to the beach."

"I got here first!" It was weak but he didn't have anything else because he *had* ridden shotgun yesterday. He looked up at his mother and he knew it was hopeless. "Okay," he mumbled and opened the door and climbed out and Clay shot through the opening and into the front seat, like a rat headed for its hole.

Aaron climbed into the back and they started for the beach. But he felt no better. In fact, if anything, he was angrier than he had been. He flopped down onto the seat, lying on his back, hoping he'd get carsick just to show her what happened when he was forced to ride in the back.

Had he been in any other position in the car he would not have seen it; a flash, a very bright flash at the top of the hill to the right of the car, and then, a very faint sound, low pitched and short. He sat up and looked out the window, marking the trees on the ridge where he had seen the flash, and then, out to sea, they heard the planes start their bombing runs on the old target hulk.

"The fighters!" Clay called out. "Hey, Aaron, the fighters are back!"

He glanced through the windshield as each plane completed its run and rose up to rejoin the formation. And then he glanced back at the hill, wishing he could see what was on top, but he was too close and the only way he'd be able to see anything was to climb up there.

They jumped out of the car in the parking lot and watched the planes circle and begin their strafing runs. Both Linda and Clay stood watching the planes, but Aaron kept his eyes focused on the hill behind them. Nothing. Just the pines blowing in the wind from the water. Maybe he hadn't really seen anything. Maybe it was just his imagination or maybe the reflection of the sun off something metal or glass. As he heard the last plane complete its run, he turned and watched it rise upward and join the other fighters, then turn to the west, and head off across the bay.

They dropped their towels and ran down to the water. The tide was full now, so they had to wade only a short way out to get wet and as soon as he dove into the salty water, Aaron forgot about the hill and what might be up there. He dove and swam and dove and splashed, as did Clay, and for a while their mother joined them and it was like old times, all of them laughing and splashing each other. Finally, Linda walked back to the beach to lie in the sun and Aaron and

Clay floated side by side, the small waves lapping over them now and then.

"I think she was murdered," Clay said.

"Yeah, me too. I think he trapped her up there, wired the door, and took away the ladder."

"It must have taken her a long time to die," Clay said.

"Probably starved to death."

"Why would he do it?" Clay asked.

"She probably made him eat his vegetables all the time when he was a kid."

Clay laughed. "Or made him pick up his clothes."

They both laughed. And then they floated along, the tide pulling them slowly out to sea, neither of them aware how far they had drifted from the beach until Aaron looked up.

"Holy cow! Look how far we drifted!"

Clay looked back toward the beach where his mother lay sleeping in the sun. She was a very long way off.

Aaron dropped down, but his feet didn't touch the bottom and he looked around at Clay. "We'd better start swimming," he said.

And though they were both strong swimmers they seemed to make very little headway against the tide and they kept having to stop and rest and each time they did, they drifted out.

"It's too far," Clay said.

"No, we're okay," Aaron said. "Just swim a little more slowly so we can last longer before we have to rest."

At first he didn't think it was going to work, but slowly he thought they were drawing closer and then bit by bit he knew they had begun to gain.

"Aaron? How much farther? I'm getting really tired."

"There's a sandbar up ahead."

"How far?"

"Not far, Clay, just keep paddling." He tried not to let his voice give away his fear and he raised his head and he could see the lighter spot about a hundred yards or so ahead. "Once we get to the sandbar we can rest and let the tide go past."

"I'm really tired, Aaron."

"You just think you are, that's all."

"I don't want to drown!"

"You're not gonna drown, Clay! Roll onto your back and float and give my your arm."

Clay flopped over and floated and Aaron took hold of his arm and began swimming sidestroke they way he had been taught in his lifesaving class back in early July. Immediately their progress slowed and for the first time Aaron wondered how long he would last.

"Clay, kick with your feet. Not hard, just enough to give me some help here."

Slowly, Clay began to kick and they began to move forward at a better pace.

"Once we get to the sandbar I think we can walk the rest of the way because the tide is going down."

"How far is it?"

"Not far." He'd lied. It was still seventy yards or more away and then as he looked toward the bar he saw a seam in the current and he understood why it was swift. The water had built up behind the bar and then swept around the end in a long arc. Past the seam the water eddied back toward the bar and now all he had to do was get them into the eddy.

"How are you doing?" Aaron asked.

"Better. I'm getting rested. A few more minutes and then I can swim on my own again."

"Just keep kicking. We're gaining on the bar all the time."

For several minutes they continued to swim and now the seam in the current had come very close and Aaron pulled a little harder and then like a boat coming from a wind-ripped sea into the calm of the harbor, they crossed the line of the current, and swam into the eddy and now the current began pulling them toward the bar.

"You can swim again now," Aaron said.

Clay rolled onto his stomach and began breast stroking alongside his brother. "What happened? We're going with the current."

"We're in an eddy behind the bar." In fact, he thought, we're there. He let his feet drift downward to touch the sand and he wondered if he had ever in his life felt anything so wonderful. "We're there! I can touch!"

A few yards later Clay's feet hit the sand, then they pulled themselves out of the water and up onto the bar where it was no more than shin deep.

"You okay?" Aaron asked.

"Just tired."

"Yeah, me too."

"Were you scared?" Clay asked.

"Yeah," Aaron said.

"I was really scared, Aaron. That current was strong."

"We were dumb not to have watched," Aaron said. "I just didn't think the water was going out so fast." He looked up ahead and he could see a whole series of bars with darker water between. But nowhere did he see a current making around the bar like the one they had just come through.

"Let's try walking and see how far we can get," Aaron said.

They walked over the crown of the bar and then the water deepened on the back side and when it got up to their necks they swam. But the current was weak and they crossed easily to the next bar and then made a game of it, going from bar to bar until they reached the shallow water that ended at the beach.

They continued walking, pushing through the warm water and then stopping to watch another round of fighter planes sweep out of the summer haze and drop to the attack.

13

Digging Steamers

They stood, watching the planes make their final dive at the old hulk and then sweep upward out of the haze and into the blue sky above, and they turned with them as they circled back in over the land and then headed out to sea, disappearing into the puffy clouds, and that's when Aaron saw the flash from the hill.

"Did you see that flash?" Clay asked.

"Yeah."

"What was it?"

"I don't know."

"Maybe we ought to check it out," Clay said.

"I don't think so."

Clay looked quizzically at his brother. "What's the big

deal?"

"What if it's the guy who shot down Captain Bayles?"

"Do you really think it could be?"

They stood looking at the hilltop. And then Aaron glanced down at the beach and the umbrella where their mother lay in the shade. And suddenly he wondered if she was all right. Why hadn't she been watching the way she always did when they were in the water? "I'm going up to the blanket."

As they walked across the open sand flat Aaron grew more and more anxious. And then, as if he somehow understood, Clay suddenly burst forward. "Race you to the blanket!" he shouted.

Aaron ran, knowing it was a lost cause, because Clay, with any head start, was just too fast. "Hey!" he shouted. "No fair!"

Clay grinned back over his shoulder and ran faster. "Try and catch me!" he shouted.

This was a game he played a lot and it was the one game he could count on winning. And anyway, the shouting had helped as his mother stirred, rolled over, and sat up.

"Do you guys have to make so much noise? I was having a great nap."

"Ooops, sorry, Mom," Clay said. "I didn't know you were asleep."

She looked out at the sandflats and then checked her watch. "Wow, I slept a long time!"

"You mean you didn't even hear the planes?" Clay looked truly astonished.

"I didn't hear a thing until you guys began to shout. Have you been in the water all this time?"

"Most of it."

"You know what I think?" she said. "I think George has probably gotten back with the motor. You ready to go?"

"Sure," Aaron said.

It took but a few minutes to gather their gear, stow it in the car, and drive to the cottage and sure enough George's truck was parked by the barn. They threw open the car doors and ran around to the back where George stood looking into the boat, sitting on the cradle, completely out of water.

"Didn't leak hardly at all," he said.

They spotted the big green outboard on the ground beside him.

"Are you gonna put the motor on?" Clay asked.

"As soon as the tide comes in, I'll move the boat down to my dock." He grinned. "How was the swimming?"

"Great," Aaron said, but he knew he hadn't hidden his anxiety over what had very nearly been a huge disaster.

But George said nothing. He nodded and then he looked up and smiled at their mother as she walked toward them. "Hi," he said.

"Hi. You got the motor, I see."

"I did. Forty horse." He shook his head doubtfully. "We'll see how it goes. This boat is bigger than I first thought. I'm thinking I should add a second motor. But what I've got in mind right now is a shellfish feed. The tide's just right for digging steamers, and then we'll go down to Orleans and buy some ocean scallops when the draggers come in. How's that sound?"

"Great!" Aaron said, Clay joining in enthusiastically.

Linda smiled. "It sounds like a lot of trouble ..."

"No, no trouble at all. It'll be fun. I love digging clams, and it's a lot more fun with company."

"Do we need to change?" Clay asked.

"Nope. You're all set. I've got the clam hooks and baskets in the truck. I thought maybe we could have this feast up at my house and that way Captain could have the pleasure of your company too."

At the beach they walked down along the edge of the great marshes to a small side creek, drained by the outgoing tide, and both Aaron and Clay began to forget how close they had come to drowning only an hour or so before.

They walked up over the sand for a way, winding ever deeper into the marsh, the reeds and eel grasses screening them from the shore, until they could only have been seen from a plane.

"Okay. Here we are," George said. "Nobody else knows about this spot, but it has the biggest and best steamers I've ever found." He pulled a clam hook from the basket. It looked like a pitchfork except that the tines had been bent forward at ninety degrees. Then he showed them how to find the clams by looking for the holes in the mud and how the steamers squirted water from the holes when you stepped near them.

He showed them how to push the fork carefully into the mud to break as few clams as possible and then they started digging. Linda dug too, ignoring the mud and the sand worms that also lived in the creek bottom. But that didn't surprise her sons. Unlike other mothers, stuff like worms and bugs didn't bother her in the least. They were there to dig clams so she dug clams.

Within a half hour they had all the clams they needed and they left the creek and walked back toward the car and the truck.

"I see the planes are back," George said. "I'm kind of surprised."

"Maybe they caught whoever shot the plane down," Clay said.

"Or maybe nobody did shoot it down," Linda said. "Maybe that hole in the cowling had been there right along."

Aaron was about to mention the flash and then it occurred to him that there might be someone watching them from the hill and it would be a dead giveaway if they all turned and looked that way.

"No, he was shot down all right," Clay said. "The smoke was coming from right behind the bullet hole."

"But how can you be sure?" his mother asked.

"I saw it."

"Got eyes like an eagle, I guess," George said.

"I didn't say I saw smoke coming out of the hole, but there was a lot of smoke was coming out of the side of the engine behind the piece of cowling with the hole in it."

"Clay's right," Aaron said. "I saw it too."

"Still," George said, "it's pretty strange that they'd risk losing another plane and perhaps this time, a pilot."

By then they had reached the car and from here the hill was hidden by the rise of the land.

"They better be careful," Aaron said. "I saw something flash from the hill up there when the planes were here and I saw it before too."

"Really?" George said. One by one he loaded the full baskets into the back of his truck. "What did it look like, exactly, Aaron?"

"Just a bright flash like a signaling mirror. The first time I thought I heard a noise but we were in the car and it could have been something else."

"What do you think it was?" Linda asked.

George shook his head and then ran his hand through his long dark hair. "Well, to tell you the truth, I don't know, but I think it's worth looking into. I'm gonna run the clams up to the house and get them into the refrigerator and clean up a little and I'll make a couple of calls. Then we'll go down to Orleans and see about those scallops. Have you guys had ocean scallops before?"

"Just bay scallops," Linda said.

"Wait till you try these. Nothing like 'em." He climbed into the truck. "I'll be about forty minutes or so."

They headed for the car and Aaron climbed into the back seat which left his brother standing with his mouth open. "You don't want shotgun?"

"No, you take it."

Clay jumped into the seat and closed the door before Aaron could change his mind. A chance like this had never turned up before and he wasn't about to ask any questions.

Aaron lay across the back seat so he would be able to see up toward the hilltop.

"Time to get the salt washed off," their mother said.

After they passed the one opening toward the hilltop, Aaron sat up and looked out over the marsh until they passed the cottage and the trees closed in on both sides. And out of nowhere he began to wonder what it would be like to live here all the time. There weren't many kids around, but then there weren't many houses around. Where would they go to school? Down in Orleans? That seemed most likely because there were plenty of people there and plenty of houses that didn't look like cottages. Out here, though, it was mostly cottages, and they would be empty once summer ended.

He thought of their neighborhood back home and how easy it was to get up a ball game with ten or a dozen other guys. They played baseball and football and hockey in the winter and sometimes even basketball, and sometimes they just sat around and talked about sports and the games they played and even … girls. They argued a lot too and sometimes the arguments even ended up in fights and some of those fights got pretty serious, especially if one of the fighters was a hothead.

If they lived here, he'd spend a lot of time with Clay and while they got into their share of disagreements, in the end, they both liked doing the same things. In a few weeks he'd be starting in the high school and it was huge and full of bullies and he'd have to watch his step constantly, keep his head down, and try not to draw any attention to himself. Would that be different here? Probably not, but at least it would be smaller. And that produced an interesting question. Why did that appeal to him? Why did he think smaller was better? He grinned to himself. Smaller meant fewer bullies, that's why. Of course, it only took one and when you were the new guy in school, it was a pretty good bet you'd draw plenty of attention. Even so, he liked the idea of going to a smaller school.

The car slowed to a stop and they climbed out, walked

down to the pond and without hesitation, dove into the crystal clear water, swimming out into the pond and then back to stand on the sandy bottom.

"Okay, guys," their mother called. "Soap time!" She tossed them each a bar of soap. "Be sure to wash your hair," she said. Then she waded in with a bar of soap and began scrubbing herself clean.

Suddenly, in the distance they heard the rumble of distant thunder, and they worked a little faster, lathering up and then diving around to get rinsed off before walking out to towel off so they could get back to the cottage before the storm hit.

14

The Paladin

The squall came boiling across Cape Cod Bay, the great black thunderheads rising impossibly high, and then it hit and for several minutes pitchforked lightning bolts spread across the sky like fireworks. Then it poured, the water driven against the house by a powerful wind. Sometimes it would let up a little and then it seemed to rain harder and then, suddenly, they could see the blue sky off to the west and the rain quickly tapered down to a soft drizzle and at that instant the storm offered one parting shot, a bolt of lightning, thick and jagged and forked at the upper end, and the thunderclap came a second behind the bolt.

"I saw it hit!" Clay shouted.

"On that hill over there." Aaron pointed to the beach.

"Right on the top!"

"It sounded like it was closer," their mother said.

"No, it was on that hill. I'm sure of it!" Clay said.

Their mother laughed. "I nearly jumped out of my skin."

"I never saw one that close before," Clay said.

As he looked out, Aaron realized that the lightning had struck on the same hill where he had seen the flash and he wondered if George had made those phone calls.

As quickly as it had come, the storm passed by, leaving the air cooler and drier.

"When will George get here?" Clay asked.

"When he does," his mother said. "But it shouldn't be much longer."

"Do we have time to go out to the barn?" Aaron asked.

"Just don't go anywhere else, I don't want to spend an hour tracking you guys down."

"We'll be right there," Aaron said.

"Let's go look at the fishing stuff."

They walked into the barn, stopping in front of the fishing gear. The rods were all short and thick, boat rods, not designed for casting even a short distance.

"You know," Aaron said, "this stuff looks like it was never used. Why would he have all this gear and never use it?"

"Isn't gear like this kind of expensive?" Clay asked.

"Yeah."

"I thought the Colemans were poor."

"Wow ... You think maybe it was stolen?"

Clay shrugged. "Actually, I hadn't thought of that. I was just trying to guess where he would have gotten the money to buy it."

"But if he stole it," Aaron said, "it might explain why he never used it."

"Because he was afraid someone would see him with it and recognize it."

"Sure."

"That's probably a pretty good guess," George said as he stood in the open door of the barn. "I remember back in the thirties there was someone who stole fishing gear from the party boats and the private boats. I'd be willing to bet that's what you're looking at."

"Wow …" Clay said.

"I've been doing some checking on Paul Coleman. I think he was a thief. The gear that's here in the barn was middle–priced stuff. But a lot of other very expensive gear went missing at about the same time. It happened here and down in Hyannis.

"My dad knew the family and he said they were all a bunch of ne'er-do-wells. The father used to steal lobsters from other fishermen's traps, or at least everyone believed he did, though they never caught him. The other brother, Mark, who was older than Paul, just disappeared. Most people think somebody shot him. It may seem strange to outsiders, but then, in the thirties, during the Depression, raiding another man's traps meant taking food from his family. Most of the men carried rifles in their boats, in fact most still do. I don't think anyone doubted that Mark Coleman got shot while raiding someone's traps. The police investigated but they never found a body and they gave it up." He sighed. "Harsh justice, but in the eyes of men who work as hard as fishermen do, perfectly reasonable and fair.

"Not too long after that the father disappeared too and all the stealing stopped. Nobody knows where he went. He just disappeared. When he left he owed people a lot of money and everyone just assumed that's why he took off."

They stood, mouths agape, as they listened to George, trying to take it all in, but it was too much to chew on all at once. It sounded more like the wild West than the East.

"Somebody really shot him?" Clay asked.

"Most likely, but no one can say for sure. Men have been lost at sea, of course, but only a handful because the fishermen here, but for a few, fish the bay and the waters close in toward shore. Even so, boats have gone down, mostly in the winter when the ice made them too heavy and they just drove into a wave and went to the bottom."

"Do you fish in the winter?" Aaron asked.

"On the good days. But I've been out in some pretty nasty weather when I had to check my traps." He shook his head. "I've been thinking that this winter I might just lie low." He grinned. "I think it's time we went down to Orleans and got those scallops. I haven't had any all summer and just thinking about them has made me hungry."

The drive seemed to take forever, as such trips always do when you aren't used to them. And it was even slower because of the summer traffic. But finally they turned onto a side road and a couple of turns later pulled up at the docks and climbed out.

They walked down the pier looking at the fishing boats, busy now with the fishermen unloading their catch in big boxes packed with ice. The strong odor of fish filled the air and now and then the ripe, rank odor of lobster bait. They stopped at a boat called the *Mary Jean*. She was nearly fifty feet long, a side trawler, and now the nets were hung in the air to dry and the big trawl doors used to hold the net close to the bottom were neatly stowed.

"H'lo, Tom," George said. "You got scallops?"

Tom Harris looked up from the deck of his boat to the pier and grinned. "Been expecting you all summer."

"Been expecting to get here all summer. Just never did."

"Couldn't have picked a better time." He pointed to a double row of burlap sacks neatly tied at the top with heavy twine. "Pricey though. Four dollars."

"Long trip?"

He grinned. "Taking 'em down to Hyannis. I'm the only boat with scallops to sell just now."

George reached into his pocket, took out some cash, and looked down at Tom. He chuckled softly. "Won't get there for nothing."

"Not much of a market here at that price," Tom said.

"Improving, though," George said and then peeled off another dollar. "Three dollars here is more profitable then four in Hyannis what with gas and time."

Tom chuckled. "I'd settle for three."

"Three it is then." He handed the bills down to Tom who stuffed them into his pocket. Then he turned, looked over the sacks, and pulled out a particularly full one. With both hands he swung it up toward George who caught it and swung it up onto the pier as if it weighed nothing.

"Thanks, Tom," George said.

"My pleasure," Tom said.

The business done, George picked up the burlap sack by the neck and they started down the pier to the car, looking once more at the boats tied up alongside the pier, and then something caught his eye and Aaron turned and looked at a boat off to his left. It had the shape of a Maine fishing boat with a high bow and a long stern with a low rail. There were lobster traps piled in neat rows from the wheelhouse to the stern, and a rack full of buoys — buoys painted exactly as the ones he'd seen in the barn — stood close to the wheelhouse. He glanced around at the other boats but he saw no other buoys like them anywhere and none with vertical stripes. The stripes were all horizontal and painted in bright colors to make them easier to see in the water.

He stopped and looked more closely, noticing that the decks were clean and no equipment had been left lying around. The boat looked as if it had been painted recently, and all in all, it didn't look a whole lot different from the other boats … except for the buoys.

"Hey, Aaron!" Clay called. "You coming?"

He glanced at the boat again, this time taking in the name painted on the stern. *The Paladin,* it said in big blocky letters. What was a paladin? Aaron glanced at the buoys and when he looked up he saw a man loom up in the hatch that led to the cabin. He was short and built like a barrel, and he had gray hair and a full gray beard. But his eyebrows were black and bushy and his unusually small beady black eyes glowed as he locked his gaze on him.

Aaron shivered. Never had he seen such a look of hatred and now his feet felt as if they had been nailed to the pier. He wanted to turn away, to run, but instead he stood there, gawking, scared, unable to break away, incapable of any movement at all.

"Hey, Aaron," Clay called. "Get a leg on, will you?"

It provided the energy he needed and yet he still had to force himself to turn his head and then, with the contact broken, he trotted off, wanting only to get away from the pure evil he had seen in those tiny eyes, than to simply catch up to the family. It was the man he had seen on the bluff.

As she drove away from the piers and the boats, Linda looked around at George. "Was three dollars a lot to pay?" she asked.

George nodded. "For Orleans, it was, but then those were the only scallops available and a man's entitled to get as much as he can. Just good business." He shook his head. "Having the only catch might happen once in three years and Tom has no choice but to take advantage of it."

"Were those all the scallops he had?" Clay asked.

"He was still bagging," George said. "I'd guess he had a lot more in his hold, probably ten times what you saw. Every now and then you get lucky. But the luck for Tom was that no one else came back with scallops."

From the back seat, Clay listened carefully to the conversation, but Aaron's mind was back at the harbor. Who was he? And why had he stared at him the way he had? He shivered, thinking that perhaps for the first time in his life he had seen someone who was truly evil and he hoped he'd never see that face again. The more perplexing question though, was what he had been doing up on the bluff the day the plane crashed?

15

Somebody Is Watching

George pulled on a pair of gloves to protect his fingers from the sharp edges of the shells and then began shucking the scallops, saving only the big muscle that opened and closed the two halves of the shell.

"This time you guys can just watch," he said as he settled onto a stool by the big double sink in the back hall. "Scallops are a little tricky and the edges are sharp and I haven't got any gloves that'll fit you."

Clay looked up at Aaron. "Where'd Mom go?"

"She's outside with Captain."

"I'll go find her." Clay pushed out through the screen door, and then stopped, trying to decide which way to turn. And then he heard his mother talking to the dog and he walked to the left, around the corner of the kitchen wing and off to where she sat on a bench looking out toward the sea, scratching Captain's ears.

The big dog heard him coming and jumped up and ran to him, his tail wagging rapidly.

Clay patted his big head and rubbed his ears and Captain stood quietly and then when Clay moved, he walked along beside him.

"He's a really nice dog," Clay said.

"He sure is," his mother said.

"I'm not afraid of him at all."

His mother smiled. "Not all dogs are mean." She picked up a ball from the bench beside her and tossed it out onto the lawn and Captain went after it full speed, scooped it up on the bounce, brought it back, and dropped it at her feet.

"Does he always do that?" Clay asked.

"He does," she said.

Clay picked up the ball and threw it as far as he could and Captain took off like a rocket, getting to the ball before it stopped bouncing. He trotted back and dropped the ball at Clay's feet.

"Tell him he's a good dog, and pet him," his mother said.

"Good boy." Clay patted the big wide head.

"But don't make him work too hard," she said. "It's pretty warm and dogs can overheat."

"How do you know so much about dogs?"

"We always had Labs, just like Captain. Your grandfather was a duck hunter, you know."

"How come he doesn't have a dog now?"

"I'm not sure. After Wishbone died, I thought he'd get

another dog, but he didn't."

"Does he still hunt?"

"That's a good question. I assumed he did, but his arthritis is pretty bad and maybe he stopped. Cold damp duck blinds aren't the best thing for arthritis, you know."

"I wish they didn't live so far away," Clay said.

"Me too."

After Clay threw the ball several more times he decided he'd like to have a dog just like Captain.

"Hey," Aaron called from the back of the house. "We're gonna go down and put the motor on the boat and move it over to the other creek. You coming?"

They walked over to the house, Captain trotting along.

"How long will it take?" Linda asked.

"About an hour." George said.

"I thought I'd get things ready for dinner."

"Great. Use whatever you need."

"I'm gonna stay and play with Captain," Clay said.

That took Aaron by surprise but he said nothing.

"Okay, then. Aaron and I will take care of the boat."

Clay and his mother watched them drive off in the old truck and then turned toward the house.

"What do you think of George?" his mother asked.

Clay shrugged. "He's pretty nice."

"Is that all?"

Again Clay shrugged. "I don't know."

"Are you sure?"

"Do you mean, do I like him?"

"Something like that."

"He doesn't talk to us like we're kids. I like that. And he

isn't bossy when he's showing us stuff. He laughs a lot too, but he doesn't laugh at me or Aaron."

"So he's maybe an all-right guy then?"

"Yeah, I guess he is."

"Yeah, I think so too."

"Does that mean you're gonna marry him?"

"Whoa, there, I never said anything like that."

"But you like him."

"I do."

"And you'd like to be married again."

"I suppose I would."

"Well, it's okay with me," Clay said. "And he's sure a lot better than those other guys you brought home."

His mother laughed.

"What's so funny?"

"Those guys were pretty terrible, weren't they?"

"Yup. And Aaron agrees with me."

"I didn't know you guys talked about stuff like this."

"Sure we do, Mom. We know lots of guys with stepfathers. Some are fine, but some of them are pretty mean. But I can tell you this. George isn't mean."

"How do you know that?"

"Because the dog that bit me comes from a family with a mean stepfather and Captain is a great dog. You can tell a lot about somebody by what kind of dog they have."

Linda smiled. "You sure can," she said.

While George lugged the motor over to the boat and slipped the mounting bracket onto the transom, Aaron began bailing out the water. And then George went up to the barn, found another can to bail with, and came back to help.

"I can't believe how much water there was," Aaron said.

"Most of it's from the rain. Later I'll rig a pump I can use with my foot so I can keep running the motor while I bail."

Scoop by scoop they lowered the water level in the boat.

"When we were down in Orleans I saw some lobster buoys ... I mean not just ordinary ones, but painted differently. They had vertical black stripes."

"Where did you see those?"

"On a boat called *The Paladin*."

"On the left as we were going out?"

"Yup."

"I noticed that boat. Very clean and well kept. I don't remember seeing it there before."

"Did you ever see buoys like those before?" Aaron asked.

"No, I can't say that I have."

"There's a whole bunch of them up in the barn. Painted just the same way."

"Now, that's curious." George scooped more water from the boat. "Looks like we're getting there."

"I think a pump is a real good idea," Aaron said.

George laughed. "I think I'll have a tarp made so when it rains the boat doesn't have to be bailed."

"What's a paladin?" Aaron asked.

"A knight errant from ancient Europe. They went from place to place offering their services to various noblemen. Twelve of them served Charlemagne, who was the King of France in the twelfth century." He stopped as he made the connection which Aaron had already made. "It's probably just a coincidence."

"I don't think so," Aaron said.

George stopped bailing. "This boat is named *The White Knight* and the pot buoys match the ones in the barn, and that boat is called *The Paladin*, which, of course, could be a white knight. Did you see the owner?"

"He's short and shaped like a barrel and he has gray hair and a big gray beard and dark little eyes."

George grinned at Aaron. "Pretty sharp eyes you've got there. I think you don't miss much."

Aaron smiled back. "My nose is even better," he said.

George began bailing. "Some might think that was a disadvantage."

"The trouble is I don't always know what it is I smell."

"Give me an example."

"Right now. There's something about the smell of this boat that I don't recognize."

"Can you describe it? I mean is it sweet or sour?"

"Like a closet."

"That's the cedar, but I'm surprised that you can smell it with all the paint and varnish."

Suddenly, the water was down to small puddles between the ribs of the boat.

"That's good enough," George said. "Hop out and untie her and I'll start the engine."

Aaron threw the line back into the boat and then stood by the bow ready to push off. The engine started on the first pull and unlike the old outboard which had no transmission, it was possible to put the drive shaft in neutral while the engine warmed.

"Okay, let's go," George said.

Aaron pushed off and climbed in over the bow and

George backed the boat out into the narrow channel until he found a small side channel and then he backed the boat into it, shifted gears, and headed out into the marsh.

For Aaron it was a great adventure, riding slowly along down the narrow creek, watching the sudden leap of egrets and heron as they rose up away from the boat. And there were other birds, too, birds he didn't recognize, and once they chased an enormous school of little baitfish, sending them leaping in huge masses to flash in the sunlight. It was impossible to take it all in, and he had no idea what most of the critters he saw were called. What he did know was that he had never been in a more exciting place, a place so full of life. And he began to think about what sorts of things lived in the water, beyond the fish and crabs. It must be endless!

They went a long way out, almost to open water, before George made a sharp turn to starboard and into a much wider and deeper creek that ran back toward the landing and his pier. And then without warning, he slowed the boat and shifted into neutral.

"I just saw the flash you were talking about," he said. "Don't turn around or whoever it is will know they've been spotted. It looked like the flash from a pair of binoculars. I saw that enough times in the war."

"Who would be watching us?"

"Could be anyone. It could even be nothing. During the war the civilian aviation spotters used that hill to watch for German planes, and it's still a popular spot for people who want a long view of the bay. Perhaps they saw us and turned the binoculars to get a better look."

"I think somebody's watching us," Aaron said.

George nodded. "Somebody is watching us right now, I think. Hard to tell for sure."

"I don't like being watched," Aaron said.

"I don't much care for it myself." George dropped the engine into forward and continued on up the creek.

They tied up the boat and George chained and locked both the motor and the boat and then stood and looked back toward the bluff.

"Is he gone?" Aaron asked.

"Can't tell." George looked at the boat. "You know, this is an exceptional boat." He pointed to the sides. "You can see how each plank is one piece from stem to stern. And if you look closely at the way everything is joined, it tells you that whoever built this was a professional. But it's not like any boat I ever saw. It looks as though someone crossed a Lyman with a Maine lobster boat." He turned away and they walked out to the road and then back to the cottage to where he had left the truck. "I'll check with a couple of old boat builders. Jason Nichols might know. I'll have to motor over there the next time I put in at Orleans. Be interesting to hear what he has to say."

By the time they got back to the house, Linda had the steamers in the pot and had found a fryer among George's pots and pans and was heating up the oil to fry the scallops she had already breaded. She had also made a salad and Clay had helped her set the table out on the porch.

"You, sir," she said, "have a very well equipped kitchen for a bachelor."

George laughed. "I had some good advice. Dad's cook, Mrs. McGinty, made a list of what I should have and I bought everything she put on the list. She's great. You'll have to meet her. Dad too. He's a little stiff, but I think you'll like him." He looked around at Aaron and Clay. "And he's got some great stories about the sea and what it took to sail a four-masted ship around the Horn."

Dinner was a rousing success with everyone talking and eating and then they all pitched in to clean up and afterward settled around the table for a fast game of slapjack, which resulted in a lot of hollering and laughing and generally rowdy behavior. In short, it was fun.

And for awhile it took Aaron's mind off the steadily increasing feelings of doom that now had begun to haunt him. Well, maybe it wasn't doom so much as just worry about where things were headed. He could not remember having even thought about the future before and suddenly it seemed never to leave his mind.

16

The Treehouse

Over the next week their lives fell into a routine that was not in the least unwelcome, reading in the mornings, afternoons on the beach; they even took several short trips over to the ocean side to swim in the surf. But the water there was much colder, so cold, in fact, that at times their feet would almost go numb.

George seemed busier now and though he turned up late most every afternoon, he'd only used the new boat once, taking it down to the boatyard in Orleans where he had another engine put on and a small steering wheel and levers to run the engines and a tarp to protect it against the rain. But what he didn't do was take them out fishing as he'd promised. The biggest change, however, was that he no longer wore cut off jeans, a short sleeved work shirt, and his old battered sneakers. Instead, he dressed in slacks and a white shirt and one time he even wore a tie and jacket. He'd also had his hair cut a lot shorter and yet despite all that, he didn't change. He still laughed and talked to them both and they still went up to his house to play with Captain, and he ate dinner with them every night.

At the cottage, he and Mom would sit at the big round table in the kitchen drinking coffee and talking and talking, though as Aaron later told Clay, it was hard to figure out exactly what they were talking about.

On rainy days, of which there were but two, they drove up to Provincetown and down to Hyannis.

By the end of that week, with George's permission, Aaron and Clay began building a tree house in the pines, using the supply of rough lumber in the barn to connect one tree with the next closest tree eight feet away by means of a bridge and then they began working on the walls and a roof. They had never done any of this before, but when they didn't know how to do something, they'd ask George and he'd draw out what they needed to know on a piece of paper. They got so absorbed in the project that each day they roared up out of bed almost with the sunrise, getting in a couple of hours of work before Linda got up to fix breakfast.

The tree house measured eight feet by four feet, and every board had to be cut by hand and it took them awhile before they began to cut the boards accurately enough so they didn't have to cut them a second time.

Putting the boards together meant a lot of bent nails had to be pulled out, but after a day or so, they got the hang of it.

Of course, a finger or two got hammered, but they learned quickly, and then, with a little practice, the pace of the work picked up considerably.

At every stage, George helped, but he didn't drive a single nail or cut even one board. He did have to show them how to mark boards on an angle so they could be cut to match the pitch of the shed roof, but at no time did he stand around and tell them what to do. When they asked, he answered.

Bit by bit the tree house came together and like all such projects it simply took time to complete. But this was Clay's kind of project and from the start he understood George's drawings because they were not so very different from the plans he built his model planes from.

After the first week, Aaron's enthusiasm began to wane. Suddenly he was tired of the work, sawing each board, climbing the ladder, and then nailing it in place and then going back to saw another board, and then sawing another board and climbing the ladder and … Three things kept him from quitting. First, Clay would not quit and there was no way he could quit if his younger brother kept going. Second, they still went to the beach every afternoon and that left him free to explore for critters he hadn't seen before. Third, each day he could see the progress. And maybe, he thought, there was a fourth part. He liked hearing George tell them what a fine job they were doing and how it was going to be the best tree house he'd ever seen.

And then, suddenly the walls were up and the roof went on and all they had left to do was tarpaper the roof. Their mother made them wait for George. It was some ten feet off the ground and while they'd certainly managed to nail on the roof boards without falling, she seemed to think that tarpapering was more dangerous.

"But Mom," Clay said as they sat eating lunch. "It's no different. It's just as high up."

"I understand that, Clay, but I still want you to wait. And you know George would be glad to help you."

Clay scowled. "We wanted to do it all by ourselves."

"You have," she said. "And it's a great job, too. You heard what George said last night."

"I wanted to have the tarpaper on by the time he got here today."

Aaron shifted the subject. "Has George quit fishing?"

"He has," Linda said, "at least commercially."

"Why?"

"Well, he decided to open a law office."

"What made him do that?"

Linda smiled. "He said he had always planned to, but just hadn't got around to it." She finished her coffee. "And today we're going to have lunch at his father's."

"In that mansion?" Aaron smiled. "I was hoping we'd get to see inside it."

"But that means we won't get to finish the roof today," Clay said.

"Don't you want to meet Captain Bean?" Linda asked.

"After we finish the roof," Clay said.

"Some things can't be put off, Clay," she said. "They just have to be done."

"Like the roof," he said.

"Does Captain Bean have a butler and a cook?"

"He does have a cook, but I don't know about a butler."

"I've never seen a butler," Aaron said.

"Will we have to get dressed up?" Clay asked.

"We will." Linda pushed back her chair and began clearing the table. "But the good news is that I didn't bring much in the way of dress clothes, so it'll be pretty casual."

"And we still have plenty to do today, Clay. We've got to finish the batten strips."

"And we have to nail the screening over the windows."

They both began lugging the dishes over to the sink.

"I'll take care of the dishes, you guys go work on your tree house."

In seconds they were out the door and climbing the ladder. They had lugged the batten strips up the day before and they began with Aaron cutting a strip and then, while Clay nailed it in place, Aaron marked and cut the next strip. For the next hour they hardly said a word and they didn't stop until they had finished the first long wall.

They sat, one to a sawhorse, looking out the windows, Clay looking off toward the cottage and Aaron staring absently across the road to where the land rose up onto higher ground. "I think Mom likes George a whole lot," he said.

"I know."

"I mean a whole, whole lot."

"Do you think she'll marry him?" Aaron asked.

"I don't know."

They sat quietly for several minutes, each of them thinking over what that would mean.

"We'd live here then," Clay said.

"I think so."

"Is that okay with you?" Clay asked.

"I don't know."

"I like it here."

They sat quietly again. In the growing heat the odor from the pitch pine grew steadily stronger and now and then a gull drifted by and from the high ground they could hear a lone crow sound off.

"Do you like him?" Aaron asked.

"Sure, don't you?"

"Yeah."

"But he hasn't taken us fishing like he promised."

"You heard what Mom said. He's opening an office."

"I like the way he doesn't boss us around," Clay said.

"I hate being bossed around."

"Mom asked me if I liked him and I told her I did. I even told her to marry him, if she liked him."

"You did?" Aaron sat with his mouth open.

"Sure. I mean, we've talked about this before, Aaron, and sooner or later we knew Mom would get married again."

"You like him that much?"

"Why not? I mean, why wouldn't I like him?"

"No reason."

"Are you saying you don't like him?"

"I'm not saying anything like that. Maybe I'm not sure I want a stepfather, that's all."

"Well, you're wrong. We should have a stepfather."

One thing about Clay, Aaron thought. He had a knack for saying what was true. They did need a stepfather. Dads just did different stuff than mothers. And then, from the corner of his eye, Aaron saw something move in the trees on the high ground across the road. At first he just watched, thinking it must be an animal of some kind, a deer maybe. George had said there were a lot of deer around. But the second time he saw it move, he knew it was human; a man, and he was standing partially hidden by the trunk of a tree as he looked down at the cottage.

Was it the same man who had been watching from the bluff the day he and George had brought the boat around? How could he get a better look at him? What could he do to get him to turn his head toward them? All he could see now was a dark profile but even that was hard to make out because of the deep shade cast by the tree.

"Okay," Clay said, "time to get back to work." He picked up a batten strip and the hammer and when he hit the nail the man turned toward the sound, froze, and watched. Only now he had turned his face into the sun and Aaron gasped softly. It was the same man!

"Come on, Aaron, I need another strip."

"There's a man watching us," Aaron whispered.

"What? Where?" Clay scrambled over next to him. "Where? Where is he?"

"Up there. In the trees."

Clay poked his face around the edge of the window opening. "Where? I don't see anything."

"See that big tree near the top? He's behind that."

"I still don't see anything."

"Just keep looking."

They heard the screen door spring squeal and the man turned his head toward the cottage and Clay saw the movement. "Now I see him! Who is he?"

"Hey you guys," their mother called. "I've got fresh lemonade for you."

"Okay, Mom," Aaron called back. "We'll be there in a minute."

"He's still there," Clay said. "What should we do?"

"I don't know."

"I wish George were here. He'd know what to do."

"Maybe we should just ignore him."

They looked up the road as they heard a truck coming but not until it cleared the rise did they recognize the iceman's truck and when they looked back the man had gone.

"Let's go," Clay said.

They climbed down the ladder and crossed the lawn.

"Should we tell Mom?" Clay asked.

"No. We'll tell George first."

"Yeah, no sense getting her all upset over nothing."

"Probably some summer guy out for a walk."

But it wasn't. It was Paul Coleman, that's who. There wasn't any question in his mind, even if it didn't make any sense. How could he possibly know who the man was? And then he remembered the lobster trap buoys in the barn and the ones he had seen on *The Paladin*. They were painted the same and that was the connection. And if Paul Coleman had killed his mother, then it seemed pretty likely that he'd kill someone else. But why? What had they done to him?

"I've seen him before," Aaron said.

"The guy on the boat in Orleans?"

"I'm pretty sure."

"Who is he?"

"I think it's Paul Coleman."

"What? I thought he was dead!"

"So did I," Aaron said. "But I can't figure out who else it could be."

"This is getting kind of scary, Aaron."

"Too scary. That's why we have to tell George. He'll know what to do."

They walked into the house and out to the kitchen.

"Took you long enough,"

They sat down at the table and Aaron covered for them. "We had one more strip to put in place," he said.

Just then the iceman knocked on the door and they both jumped like startled rabbits.

17

Lunch At Captain Bean's

Captain Elijah Nickerson Bean took them by surprise. They had expected an old man, and he certainly was old, but somehow he neither looked nor acted the way they had come to think old men should act. He was almost as tall as his son and he had a full head of gray hair and his hands and face displayed the lines and wrinkles that come with age, but he stood very straight and he walked with a quick step and in the dim light of the huge foyer of the big old house, his pale gray eyes flashed warmly as he greeted his guests.

"Welcome," he said, "George told me a great deal about you all, and I confess, I've been most eager to meet you."

He waited until Linda offered her hand and then took it immediately, smiling at her and she could feel his eyes evaluating what he saw. He seemed pleased, for his smile never wavered and then he turned to Aaron and Clay. He shook hands with them, each offering a strong grip in return, just as they'd been instructed by their mother.

"Well, what fine lookin' young men you both be."

They smiled, relaxing just the least little bit, but still on guard. You were never quite certain how to act with any adult, but old people posed some particular problems in the way they held to certain behavioral expectations when it came to kids. But they saw none of that in Captain Bean.

"I have an idea," Captain Bean said, "you might like a tour of the house, so I'm going to leave that to George and I'll drop anchor in the library. Georgette and Carey are due in a half hour, and it shouldn't take much more than that to cover the main deck." He looked at Linda. "I apologize for not leading the inspection, but my old knees prefer sittin' to standin' nowadays."

"We'll join you in the library, Dad," George said. "I suspect these young fellas here would like to hear a story or two about the old days of iron men and wooden ships."

Captain Bean smiled. "I guess I can manage that all right, but you have to promise not to be too bored. Man gets old, he gets garrulous. No escapin' that."

They began the tour in the living room and headed straight for the enormous ship model, standing several feet tall with its four masts flying a full set of squarish sails.

"Wow," Clay said, "now that's what I call a ship model!" He walked around it, soaking up detail after detail. "This is amazing. It must have taken forever to build it!"

"This was Captain Benjamin Bean's square rigger,"

George said. "He sailed it all over the world. When he retired, his son, Fairchild, who was my grandfather, took over the company. They had three ships by then."

They left the living room and walked into another room with yet another model of a big square rigger. "This was Captain Fairchild's ship. He made captain by the time he was twenty-one, sailing for a different owner and then he took command of this ship when it was new. Of course times changed and the company changed with the times, gradually going from sail to steam. But it took a while and my father first went to sea on a four-masted schooner."

In yet another room, they stood before a model of a steam powered freighter. "This was the first boat Dad captained. By then the company fleet numbered ten vessels. That lasted until my mother died and then Dad sold to another, bigger company, and Bean and Company disappeared. Till then the family had only summered on the Cape because the business was all in Boston and New York. But after the company had been sold we moved back here.

"I grew up here until I was 12 and then I was sent to boarding school. But I spent my summers here and I always hated leaving. Everywhere else seemed sort of like weak tea compared to the Cape. Dad had a great many other business interests and he traveled much of the time and it was better being away at school than here with only the housekeeper. My sisters are both much older, and they married before I finished boarding school. Dad wanted me to go to Harvard, but by then I hated cities and I chose Bowdoin instead."

"I don't think I'd like to go to boarding school," Aaron said.

"Me either," Clay said.

"I can't say I much cared for it," George said, "but it was better than being here then."

He stepped out into the hall, crossed, and pushed open the French doors to yet another room. "This is the trophy room, and I guess you can see why it's called that."

From every wall hung the heads of animals; lion, kudu, water buffalo, deer, elk, caribou, moose. The full head and skin of a Bengal tiger lay spread across the floor and a complete grizzly stood at one end of the room, his enormous teeth bared, his giant claws spread.

"One of Dad's favorite tricks is to bring someone who hasn't been here before through the doors by the bear and watch them jump out of their skin." He smiled. "There's a heck of a story behind that bear, but I'll let him tell you."

Aaron and Clay walked slowly around, trying to absorb what they saw, their eyes wide, their mouths open.

"Your father shot all of these?" Clay asked.

"He did. Dad has traveled to every continent a number of times and because of his business he has known some of the most famous men in the world and he's hunted with most of them at one time or another."

"Have you hunted in any of those places?" Aaron asked.

"No. Just here on the Cape. The war came along about the time I finished college and I had learned how to fly, so I joined the Navy."

"My father would love to see this," Linda said. "He's hunted all his life, but always for birds. And he always had Labs like Captain. I know he wanted to go to Africa, but he could never justify the time away from his practice. He just couldn't leave either his patients or his students for that long."

"Where did he teach?"

"Johns Hopkins. He's retired now ... well, mostly retired. He still consults, of course, and he lectures now and then. He and Mother prefer to spend their time in what used to be our summer house down on the Chesapeake. They live there full time now. But his hunting days are mostly over, I'm afraid. Arthritis."

"It would be hard to give up hunting. There's nothing like watching your dog work a patch of cover." He shook his head. "Nothing like it." He shook his head again and looked at his watch. "Time to head for the library," he said. "Dad will be waiting and my sisters should be here and Dad'll be looking forward to a martini. He only has one drink a day now and he smokes two cigars a day and curses because Doctor Margolis says he shouldn't even have those. The way he sees it, what harm can they do to someone who's eighty-seven?" He grinned. "I expect he has more than two."

They trooped down the hall and into the library and then the trial began. Sitting. Listening to adults. Having to smile and be polite but mostly being bored beyond anything. But Georgette and Carey smiled and didn't ask any of the dumb questions adults always ask like, "How is school?" which was the dumbest question you could ask any boy.

Aaron and Clay sat on the love seat, trying to listen, and fidgeting, looking out the windows, looking around the room, like some sort of beasts trapped in a zoo. Even so, it was their mother who got bombarded with questions and yet she didn't seem to mind, smiling, making little jokes, and all they could do was sit there, getting itchier by the second.

And then, as if he had been reading their minds, George stood up and walked over to them.

"We've got a little time before lunch, why don't you guys follow me? I've got something I want to show you."

They were up and gone in seconds, following George out through the back of the house to the big barn.

"Not so long ago," George said, "nobody here had cars and everyone traveled by horse and carriage."

They followed him into the barn, stopping by an enclosed four-wheeled carriage.

"This is the last one I know of and the only one that gets driven regularly. Not that Dad is old fashioned. He's got three cars and he loves any machine that was ever made, but he keeps this carriage and a team of horses and Charlie Neal, the man who takes care of the grounds and drives Dad where he wants to go, also drives the carriage. It makes quite a sight and holds up traffic something awful, but Dad says it gives him a way to stay in touch with the past."

"Can we get in?" Clay asked.

"Sure, climb all over it."

They tried the inside of the carriage and then climbed up onto the driver's seat and then jumped down and examined the wheels and the axles and everything else that moved.

"Wow," Aaron said. "It looks like it's brand new."

"Charlie treats it just that way. I think he gets as big a kick out of driving it as Dad does riding in it."

"Where are the horses?" Aaron asked.

"Right down there in the stalls."

They walked that way, stopping at the first stall, and then the next where the second of the two sleek black geldings quietly munched his hay. He raised his head and looked at them and then shook himself and went on chewing.

"Our Grandpa Harrison has horses," Aaron said. "He uses them for hunting."

"Where does he live?"

"In Virginia."

"So your whole family comes from the South, then?" George asked.

"That's where he and Gramma retired to. They used to live in Connecticut but they love to ride and they wanted a shorter winter."

"What did your grandfather do in Connecticut?"

"He was president of some big company that made planes, I think," Aaron said.

"Quite a family," George said.

"Oh yeah," Clay said. "We got doctors and lawyers and company presidents and even a judge."

"But no sea captains," Aaron said. "My father was the first to ever go to sea, and that was because of the war. He was a submarine captain and … hey! We do have a sea captain in the family!"

"You certainly do," George said. "And one heck of a sea captain, as I recall."

"You knew our father?" Clay asked.

"I knew of him. He was a pretty famous guy in the Navy. Played absolute hob with the Japs."

"Wow, I didn't know that," Aaron said. "I knew he was a hero but I didn't know anyone else knew."

"Let me ask you guys a question, off the subject. Has anything strange been happening at the cottage?"

"A man was watching us today when we were working on the tree house."

"Did you recognize him?"

"Aaron got a good look at him."

"It was the same man I saw on that boat, *The Paladin*. And I saw him before that. It was the day the plane crashed and he was standing on the bluff watching. I saw him and then I looked away and when I looked back he was gone."

George nodded. "Has he come close to the cottage?"

Aaron shrugged. "He could have, at night."

"Let's go back inside. I need to make a phone call."

"Do you think he'll try to get in?" Clay asked.

George smiled. "I don't think so. I don't think he wants any trouble, but I'm not happy that he's been watching. I'm going to get all new locks on the cottage. The barn is secure enough with the new padlocks, but the house locks are ancient. I think they're the original locks."

"Will we be all right there?" Clay asked.

"I'll make sure of it," George said.

18

Blues

"How seaworthy are you guys?" George asked as he sat at the table, holding his cup of coffee.

"Seaworthy?"

Linda chuckled. "He means do we get seasick and tl answer is no. We've all spent a considerable amount of tin on the Chesapeake in all kinds of weather."

"Good. Then we can go for blues. We'll be fishing in a r and the water gets pretty churned up after it goes over tl bar. Depending where we are in the tide, and how much wir there is and which direction it comes from, the water in tl rip can get downright desperate. I've seen it run six-fo waves, though most of the time the waves run three to fo feet. You can't anchor in that, so we'll be trolling up agair it and then dropping back down and going into it again. Wrecker's Rip they call it and you don't fish there without a good sound boat, and that we have. When I brought the boat back from Orleans I went out and put her into the rip to see what she'd do and she handled the water easily. In fact, that boat will handle just about any water.

"But the even better news is that there are a lot of blues around. They were there in the rip when I tested the boat, but I didn't have a rod with me. But they were there and feeding because the gulls were there. For blues you watch the gulls, not the terns. When they're feeding, the blues chop into the bait and pieces of fish rise to the surface for the gulls to fight over."

"How big are these fish?" Aaron asked.

"They go as high as twenty pounds but fish that size are pretty rare. The schools here are mostly smaller. Eight-pound fish are common, though now and then you'll get into a school of fish that go up to fifteen and sixteen pounds," he said. "But get ready, because these fish can fight."

"How long will we be out?" Linda asked.

"Depends on how well we do, but if it's slow, then probably till the ebb."

"Then we won't need a lunch."

"Just something to drink."

Within a half-hour they had finished breakfast and closed up the house.

"How do the new locks work?" George asked.

"They work fine," Linda said, and then she said something more, but neither Aaron nor Clay heard because they had raced on down the road to the boat. It looked a lot different. A console now jutted out from the starboard side near the stern, and it held a steering wheel, throttle levers, and levers to shift gears. And a small deck had been built up at the bow, extending back about three feet, providing a place to store gear. By the time George and Linda arrived they had looked over the rods, noting that they were already rigged and that only increased their eagerness.

"What took you guys so long?" Clay called. "Those fish won't wait forever."

George laughed. "Just hold your horses, we've got a slow ride out. There's only just enough water to make it. Half-hour ago, we'd couldn't have gotten out. We may still have to pole in a couple of places." He stepped into the boat, reached under the foredeck and produced four life vests. "I know nobody ever wears these, but in my boat everybody wears one. Just like the Navy. When you're on deck you wear a vest."

If he had expected resistance, he got none.

Right from the start, they had to pole the boat down the long narrow creek until it merged with yet another creek, and then George ran with one motor cocked up and silent and held the second motor partially up out of the water to keep the prop from digging into the creek bottom. Even so it left a long plume of mud in the wake behind.

When they finally turned into the main creek, he lowered the second motor, pulled the cord, and then with both motors going, *The White Knight* leaped forward, coming quickly up into a plane, the hull coming up out of the water as they skimmed along around the wide turns and finally broke out into the open bay.

With the winds light and blowing from the southwest, the waves seemed more like ripples and the big boat roared along, heading for the reef some two miles out. And because the water was so calm, they could see the rip from a long way off, looking completely improbable as the water leaped and churned where the incoming tide came boiling over the bar. And as they drew closer, Aaron began to wonder whether the water would just swallow them up.

"I don't remember seeing anything like that in the Chesapeake," Clay said.

"They're there," Linda said, "but we always give them a wide berth."

George brought the boat in well below the rip and then swung the bow up into the current. "Okay, grab the poles," he said. "Let out line till you feel the jig hit the bottom, then crank in about ten feet. The idea is to pull up on the rod and jerk the jig toward the surface and then let it fall back. Usually they hit on the upward pull, but when they're really feeding, they'll hit anything moving. When someone gets a fish on, we'll slide out of the rip until we get the fish aboard."

Aaron let the jig drop into the water, feeling the boat surge upward as it hit the first of the big waves and rose upward. He grinned. "This is gonna be fun!"

Clay dropped his jig over. "How big did you say they are?" he asked.

"Most likely five to eight pounds and up. Now, once you feel a fish hit, jerk up hard on the rod to set the hook. Blues are tough fish and they've got a lot of fight, especially in this kind of current." He adjusted the speed of the boat, slowing it to make sure the jigs could get to the bottom, and then held a steady speed. "Stay ready," he said and watched as Aaron and Clay, operating from opposite sides of the boat, began the process of twitching the jigs upward and then letting them drop.

"If we don't get anything at this depth, we'll shorten the lines on the next run. The bigger fish are usually closer to the bottom, but with blues it depends on where the schools of bait are."

Slowly the waves grew larger and it was strange to ride up in the broad band of roiled water and look out at the calm water of the bay just a short distance away, but it was also great fun to feel the surge and plunge of the boat over the waves.

"Wow!" Clay shouted as his rod dipped down and he jerked up hard just the way he'd been told. "I got one!"

And then Aaron shouted as a fish hit his jig too. "This is a big fish! I mean a really big fish!"

George throttled down the engines, keeping the bow into the current but slowly letting the boat drift off to the right and away from the rip, toward the slack water where it would be easier to fight the fish.

And it was a fight. Blues are tough and unrelenting. They can sound for the bottom, or rip huge amounts of line in long, straight, unstoppable runs. They can also shoot to the surface and leap into the air. More importantly, they fight with everything they have for as long as they can last. Both stout boat rods bent hard as the fish ran from the pressure of the line.

George laughed. "We're into 'em, all right. And they're big!" He watched each rod. "Tighten your drag," he called to Clay. "It's stripping out too fast."

Clay turned the big metal starlike wheel just inboard of the reel handle and the line slowed in going out, but the rod bent more fiercely downward.

Aaron increased the drag on his reel and focused on the line, now hissing through the water. Bit by bit they pumped the rods and reeled in line, and while neither of them had ever caught fish this large, they had caught plenty of fish and they knew what to do.

"You guys are good," George said. "Absolute pros."

It took about forty minutes for the fish to tire and by then both boys had begun to show the strain. George shifted the engines into neutral and throttled down to idle and then stood and picked up the gaff. Aaron's fish surfaced first and the size of it nearly caused his eyes to pop out of his head.

With a slick, well-practiced motion, George slipped the hook on the gaff up under the gills and jerked the fish into the boat. "Look out for the teeth," he said. "Just let him lie until we boat Clay's fish."

Less than a minute later Clay's fish broke the surface, but only for a second and then he dove for the bottom, but Clay leaned back into the rod and this time the fish turned back toward the surface. Once again George gaffed the fish and hauled it into the boat.

"Now those are two fine fish!" George said, "And you guys fought 'em like you'd been doing it all your lives." He bent over the fish. "When you take the hook out of a blue, it's best not to get your fingers too close." He pulled a long handled pliers from his pocket, closed the jaws around the hook and twisted it free of Aaron's fish and then did the same with Clay's. Then he produced a long-bladed knife and ran the blade through the head of each fish, killing them. Both boys wound in line and hooked the lure to the first guide on the rod as they looked at the two huge fish on the bottom of the boat.

"Those are big blues," George said. "Fifteen pounds at least." He dropped the engines into gear, opened them up and ran back to the beginning of the rip. "You guys ready?" He laughed. "Stupid question." He looked forward to where Linda sat watching. "You gonna fish?"

"Not for those monsters. I'll leave that to the menfolk."

"Okay then, let 'em go."

The jigs shot downward into the current and before they hit bottom both boys were hooked up.

This time George, holding the rod with one hand, dropped a jig just off the stern and he hooked up immediately. "How about that!" he shouted, sounding very much as if he'd gone back to being a boy no older than either Aaron or Clay.

An hour later they had five fish in the boat and they headed back into the rip. But this time they trolled right up to the reef before they reeled in and ran back down to make another pass. George brought the boat up along the edge of the rip and once again they all hooked up.

It was the last run. By the time they had boated the fish, their muscles were so tired, neither Aaron nor Clay could hardly lift their arms.

"Okay," George asked, "ready to quit? We can come back another time. There're almost always fish here."

Aaron looked at Clay and waited, and then looked back

at George. "My arms feel like lead."

And that left Clay free to follow his brother's lead without looking like a sissy. "Me too," he said. "But I never had so much fun fishing in my life!"

"Me either!" Aaron said. "Just look at the size of those fish!"

"How will we eat all them all?" Linda asked.

"We'll keep one to eat, two for smoking and then the rest I'll take to the fish market. Good market for blues just now with all the summer people here and not many blues being caught. They sort of disappear for a while in the middle of summer and then about now they turn up." He shook his head. "They're a wonderful fish. Fun to catch and great eating, especially when they're grilled out."

He sat down, put the engines in gear and then opened up the throttles as they headed back across the bay. The wind had come up some and now the boat threw the spray to the sides as it flattened the waves.

Before they reached the creek, George brought the boat up into the lee of one of the small islands and dropped the anchor. "Time to clean the fish," he said. He set a long board crosswise of the boat, extending from gunwale to gunwale, picked up a fish and then with his long filleting knife, started at the tail and in what seemed like seconds he had scaled the fish and cut one huge slab from each side. He tossed the carcasses overboard. "Usually I'd save the remains for lobster bait, but I've only got a few traps out now and I've got plenty of bait. The crabs will make short work of what's left."

He talked a steady stream as he worked, and he showed them how to rinse the fillets in the water pail, emptying it after each pair had been washed. "We want to get all the blood off," he said. "The blood spoils first."

Finally, with the fillets cleaned, he held the fish board over the side and scrubbed it down with a wire brush. "And that just about does it. What's more, I'm getting hungry and I've a fridge full of cold cuts for sandwiches, which I expect might just hit the spot about now."

As they drove into the yard, Captain came bounding from the porch to meet them, and Clay thought as he played with the big black dog that this was as close to heaven as anyone was likely to get.

19

The Trap

Aaron woke in the flat dark of the night just before the light began to billow up out of the east, listening to a sound he didn't recognize. He lay on his back, letting his eyes adjust and listening to the gentle grating that came and went. He counted the intervals and found that at times it was regular and at other times irregular.

Then Clay spoke. "Are you hearing that?" he asked.

"Yeah."

"What is it?"

"I don't know. Something blowing in the wind maybe."

"It sounds like it's far away," Clay said.

"Which way do you think?"

"To the far side of the house."

"By the barn?"

"Yeah, maybe somebody's trying to break into the barn."

Aaron climbed out of bed, walked to the window, and looked out. "I can't see a thing."

"I'm glad George had those new locks put on the cottage," Clay said.

"Why would anyone break into the barn? Most of what's in there is a bunch of junk."

"So, let him have it."

"You mean just let him break in?"

"What else can we do?" Clay asked. It was so dark in the room he couldn't see his brother even when he stood by the window.

"If there was nothing worth stealing why did George put the padlocks on it?"

"It was the police. They said it had to be locked until they finished their investigation."

"I didn't hear that."

"I did. I was standing right there."

"But why would somebody want to break into the barn now after it was left open for who knows how long?"

"Got me," Clay said.

"Maybe we should go downstairs and look out the kitchen window. Maybe we can see something. But even if we can't, we'll know where the sound is coming from."

"You go," Clay said.

"Com'on, Clay. There's nothing to be afraid of."

"Yeah there is. Whoever's trying to break into the barn."

"But we're inside the house."

"So what? Bad guys go right through doors."

"But he can't see in the dark any better than we can."

Aaron picked up his shorts from the floor and pulled them on. "I'm gonna check."

"Go ahead."

Aaron pulled on his sneakers and stood up.

"Wait," Clay said. "I'm coming with you." He didn't want to, but neither did he want to be left up here alone. He hopped out of bed, dressed, and they headed down the stairs, moving very slowly so they wouldn't make the least sound, feeling their way along through the dark.

They crossed the main room and then stepped into the kitchen and walked toward the window, keeping low until they could stand against the wall and peek around the window frame. Slowly they eased their heads around to where they could see and then waited. In just the time it had taken them to get downstairs, the sky had begun to lighten in the east but it offered little help as the fog that had moved in from the marsh was so thick that the barn showed only as a dark smudge.

"Can you see anything?" Clay asked.

"Nothing."

"I don't hear the sound anymore."

"Me either."

Just then the sound came again, a steady metallic rasping clearly coming from the front of the barn.

"It sounds like something being sawed," Clay said.

Aaron listened and strained his eyes against the fog, trying to make his mind see what his eyes could not. But it was no use. He couldn't connect the sound with anything he had heard before.

"I know what it is," Clay said. "He's trying to saw the lock off the barn."

"Are you sure?"

"Positive."

On the other hand, Aaron thought, Clay was always positive about everything. And yet, now, the longer he listened, the more convinced he grew that Clay was right. In his imagination he could even see the saw blade moving back and forth. "I didn't know there were saws that could cut metal."

"Hacksaws."

It had, by then, grown lighter still and suddenly they could see the fog swirl as a breeze came up from the marsh. Then Clay moved to change his position so he could see better and when he stepped back his foot collided with a small end table and the books sitting on the flat surface cascaded onto the floor with a considerable thump. The sound of the sawing stopped. They waited and listened and now they could hear no sound at all beyond the breeze which had become a wind.

"I think he's gone," Clay said.

"Shhh. Listen."

They stood silently, straining to hear, but now there was only the voice of the wind whistling softly in the eaves of the old house as it drove the fog away, leaving the flat dark of early morning behind.

"Maybe the sound of the books falling scared him off," Aaron said.

Then, down the road they heard a car start up and drive away. Aaron crossed the kitchen, found the flashlight, and walked toward the back door, stopping and looking back at

Clay. "You coming?"

"You're going outside?"

"You heard the car drive off."

"Maybe it wasn't his car," Clay said. "Maybe he's waiting for us out there in the dark."

Aaron walked over to the fireplace and wrapped his hand around the heavy poker. "This ought to even things up," he said.

"What will?"

"I took the poker from the fireplace." He opened the door and turned on the flashlight and Clay scooted across the room and got in behind him.

They stepped outside, the yellow beam from the light working like a crow bar, prying apart the dark. Step by step they inched closer to the front of the barn, listening for the faintest sound, but hearing nothing beyond the soft whistle of the wind.

As soon as the light struck the big padlock it was clear that somebody had been trying to cut away the lock. But it was also clear that either they had a very dull hacksaw or the metal in the lock was especially hard. Only a thin line showed on the loop in the lock where it passed through the ring on the hasp that came through the door from the inside.

"Look at that," Aaron said, pointing to the saw mark on the lock.

"I told you. He was using a hacksaw."

"That's what it looks like."

Clay shivered. "I wish we had a telephone."

Aaron shone the light at the ground, looking at the foot tracks in the damp sand. "Either he's got really small feet, or it's a kid."

"Should we wake up Mom?" Clay asked.

"Naw, he won't be back and we can tell George in the morning. He'll know what to do."

"What makes you think he won't be back?"

"Because we ran him off."

"I wish I could be sure of that," Clay said.

"He won't come back." Aaron turned toward the house, hoping Clay believed him.

Clay walked alongside him and then jumped ahead when they got to the door. It felt a lot safer inside.

They walked back upstairs to their room and Clay took off his sneaks and shorts and climbed into bed. But Aaron decided to stay the way he was and simply lay down on the covers, keeping the flashlight close by his side, wondering why he felt more angry than afraid.

"Clay?"

"Yeah?"

"Don't tell anyone about this, okay?"

"Not even Mom?"

"No one."

"Why?"

"I'm gonna set a trap."

"What kind of a trap?"

"I don't know yet, but I'll think of something."

"Then you think he's coming back and you were lying before."

"No, I just wanna be on the safe side, that's all."

"Can I help?"

"Sure."

"Okay, I won't say anything."

But as he lay on his bed, his hands resting by his sides, Aaron could not imagine what sort of trap he could set. Part of the problem was that he hadn't exactly spent a lot of time thinking about how you trapped anything. All he could remember were the few small animal traps he'd seen in the Boy Scout Handbook and somehow he didn't think they'd work when it came to trapping a human being.

As he considered the possibilities, he listened, his head resting on the pillow, but all he could hear was the sound of Clay's slow steady breathing and the whisper of the wind in the screens covering the open windows.

In the morning he and Clay went out and unlocked the barn and began prowling around, re-examining all the neat stuff. But now he was looking for something in particular, without knowing exactly what he was looking for.

"Do you think George knows how to build a lobster pot?" Clay asked.

"Sure. I think he knows everything."

"I sure hope Mom lets us get a dog like Captain."

"Maybe, if we lived in a place that wasn't so crowded," Aaron said.

"I like it here," Clay said.

"Were you serious about Mom marrying George? I mean you really think he'd be an okay stepfather?"

"I told you that."

"I wanted to know whether you'd changed your mind."

"Do you think it might happen?"

"I think Mom likes him a lot."

"Yeah, me too."

For a while they said no more, concentrating on prowling around, trying to see what they had not seen before. Aaron spoke first. "This would be easier if we get inside the mind of the guy who's trying to get in here."

"How could you do that?"

"Imagination."

"Sometimes you have some strange ideas, Aaron, you know that?"

"Okay. Suppose it's Paul Coleman."

"Except that he's dead."

"But we don't know that for sure. No body was ever found."

"How creepy is this going to get?" Clay asked.

Aaron laughed. "All we have to do is think like someone who murdered his mother."

"Right. Nothing to it."

"I didn't say it would be easy."

"How about impossible?" Clay looked over at the workbench, wondering if that wolf spider was still around.

"Suppose he was alive and heard that the body had been found. Maybe he left something here that could connect him to the murder. Wouldn't he come back to try and get it?"

"Not if he was smart. If he was smart he would stay disappeared."

"But nothing we know about the Colemans says that any of them were smart."

Clay sighed. He hated stuff like this. No facts. No proof. It was why he hated English in school. With math and science you had facts. But he also knew that once Aaron's imagination got going there would be no stopping him until he came up with some strange theory and then began to believe it.

"I think that's what happened," Aaron said.

"How do you prove it?"

"I don't know yet. I need to figure out what he came back for."

"Let's think about something else. What we were talking about before."

"You mean Mom marrying George?"

"Yeah."

"Like what?"

"Well, would we move here?"

"Probably. Why wouldn't we?"

"I don't know."

"George has a house here and family."

"And you think Mom likes him?"

"I'm pretty sure."

"Does he like her?"

"We sure see a lot of him."

"But I don't know much about stuff like that. I think you have to be a girl to figure out stuff like that."

Aaron laughed and looked around at Clay smiling back at him. For a guy who was only twelve, his brother said some funny stuff. "Well, I think we better be prepared," he said.

"Do you like it out here?"

"It's the most interesting place I've ever been."

"Yeah. Planes falling out of the sky, a skeleton in a rocker and now somebody trying to break into the barn in the middle of the night, digging clams, fooling around with boats and motors, and never mind how great the fishing is."

And just then Aaron spotted the big fishing net hanging from the ceiling. Perfect. Absolutely perfect. And now all he had to figure out was how to rig it.

"What are you looking at?" Clay asked.

"That net. It'd make a perfect trap."

Clay craned his head back to look up at the net. "How would you do it?"

"I don't know. What do you think?"

"We could lay it on the floor and when he stepped into it the net would come together and trap him inside. I saw that in the movies once."

"So what we have to figure out is how to make that work. It'll be dark and he won't dare turn on a light right away, so he'd walk right onto the net."

Bit by bit they started to hammer out their plan. And then, once things started to fall into place, they went to work. They began by climbing up the ladder and installing a pulley on the central beam some ten feet above the floor and then running a rope through the pulley and attaching it to the corners of the net. Then they got a block and fall and hauled the concrete block that had been used to keep the attic door closed over to the front of the barn.

"The ceiling isn't high enough," Clay said.

"Maybe we can do it outside. Come here." Aaron stepped outside and pointed to a large beam that stuck several feet out from the front of the building above the single door into the loft of the barn. "We could hide the net under the sand out there and use that beam. It's even got a big pulley on it already."

"And then," Clay said, "we could hoist the block up against the ceiling and run a wire to the outside so that when he stepped into the wire the block would fall and pull the net up and trap him inside."

"I always knew you were a genius," Aaron said. "That's exactly what we'll do."

They carried one of the ropes that George had brought upstairs and then climbed into the loft. It was the first time they had been up there since the body had been removed and they were a little spooked but, with the trap on their minds, they recovered quickly, walked to the front of the barn and opened the loft door.

"How are you gonna get the rope through the pulley?" Clay asked.

"See the way it's made? You don't have to push the rope through, you can slip it over the side." He looked around, spotting a batten strip about ten feet long. "I'll use that."

"There's a second pulley," Clay said.

"Perfect. You go pull the ladder up and we'll get the rope through the pulleys. Then we'll have to cut a hole in the floor to let the rope through."

"We'll have to run the net rope to the side or he'll see it," Clay said. He stopped and scratched his head. "That means the net won't go up very high because the slack rope can only be about eight feet, unless we cut another hole through the barn floor."

Aaron smiled. "How do you figure out stuff like that? I'd have had to try it to find that out."

Clay shrugged. "And we'll have to use a really strong rope on the block or when it stops, it'll break the rope."

"Is the rope that George brought down strong enough?"

"The block has to weigh more than the weight of the net and the guy in it." He drew a picture in his mind of the block dropping and the net coming up. "The rope doesn't have to be as strong as I thought because once the net starts up, it'll slow the speed of the falling block. I think George's rope will be plenty strong enough."

By the time their mother called them for lunch, they had cut a hole in the floor of the loft and another hole in the floor of the barn, which they rigged with a trap door. Finally, using the block and fall, they hoisted the block up into the loft and eased it onto the floor next to the hole.

"We'll go out after dark and bury the net," Aaron said, "then we'll set the trap and wait."

"Do you think it'll work?"

"Of course it'll work. But we ought to test it with something lighter than that big block, something that might not break the rope."

"Good idea. Let's go get lunch before Mom comes looking for us. We don't want her to see this."

"Yeah," Aaron said. "It might be kind of hard to explain, huh?"

20

Discoveries

After lunch they headed for the beach and for a while Aaron and Clay worked on a huge sand castle, complete with tunnels and turrets. By the time they had completed that, the tide had gone fully out and they grabbed a bucket and the two clam hooks.

"You coming, Mom?" Aaron asked.

"No, I'm going to read. I'll help with the quahogs when you get back."

They walked off down along the edge of the marsh, trying to find the little creek that George had showed them, and were somewhat surprised when they couldn't find it.

"We should have watched more closely," Aaron said.

"I thought it was right about here," Clay said.

"There sure are a lot of them," Aaron said.

"We should have marked it."

"Maybe we can try a different one." Aaron pointed to a narrow slot that led back up into the marsh which now on the low tide was almost completely dry.

"Okay with me," Clay said.

They walked back up along the narrow passage, stopping now and then to dig, but finding nothing. The high grasses along the banks slowly closed them in until they couldn't see the surrounding marsh at all, and the sun, blazing down, grew hotter with the cooling breezes cut off by the grasses. But they found clams, in fact, plenty of clams and once they began digging, they ignored the heat. They dug and dug until they had filled the bucket and then they turned and started back and that's when Clay spotted something in yet another side creek.

"That looks like a boat," he said.

They walked up into the creek, keeping to where the sandy bottom was hard enough to keep from sinking. It was, in fact, a boat, very old and mostly rotted where it stuck out above the mud.

"I wonder how long it's been here?" Aaron asked.

"A long time. But how did it get here?"

"Maybe it blew up in a big storm when the marsh was flooded."

They walked around the boat and Aaron stopped at the stern and began digging away the mud.

"What are you doing?" Clay asked.

"Trying to see if the boat has a name."

Clay grabbed the clam hooks and handed one to his

brother. "This'll be faster," he said.

Minutes later they had cleared the mud away and then Aaron scooped some water and threw it against the transom and they could make out the name. *The Queen's Pawn.*

"Wow, look at that!" Aaron said. "It's another chess piece. *The Black Queen, The White Knight* and now *The Queen's Pawn.* I think maybe the Colemans weren't so dumb after all. They must have been at least smart enough to play chess."

"You think this is one of their boats?"

"Sure it is. Don't you see how it fits?"

"I guess so. But I don't know what it means."

"The mother was the black queen, Paul was the white knight and his brother must have been the queen's pawn."

"What about the father?"

"That hasn't turned up yet. But now we need to dig up this boat and find out whether it's damaged."

"Why?" Clay asked, thinking that digging the boat out was gonna be an awful lot of hard work.

"Because the Colemans were supposed to have been lost at sea. But if this boat isn't damaged, then maybe they weren't. And if they weren't, then maybe something else caused them to disappear."

"Okay, but we can't do it now. The tide'll be coming in pretty soon and we promised Mom we'd dig quahogs for a chowder."

"We'll need to mark the main creek we came up so we can find it again."

They walked back out to where the marsh ended and then as they walked back toward the beach, they counted the little creeks that drained the marsh. Leaving the clams in the water where they would stay fresh, they walked up to the blanket to get their mother.

"You guys ready to go for the quahogs now?"

"We got plenty of steamers," Clay said.

"Do we need the clam hooks?" their mother asked.

"No. We find them with our feet," Aaron said.

From the start it was fun, as clamming almost always is. But it's especially nice to dig them when the water is warm and you have to squat down into it to pull the big quahogs free of the sandy mud.

Even Clay got into it this time, ignoring what other strange creatures might be lurking in the mud. With three of them digging, they filled the basket easily and then, later, sitting back on the blanket with the tide creeping steadily in to cover the flats, Clay turned toward his mother. "Where's George today?"

"He told me last night he had to go down to Hyannis on business. He said he'd be back by late afternoon."

"He's really giving up fishing, isn't he?" Aaron asked.

"He is," she said.

"I like him better as a fisherman," Clay said.

"I think he needs something more. Sometimes smart people need to work at more complicated things."

"That's why he plays chess," Aaron said. "Nothing makes you think more than chess."

"Chess is a dumb game," Clay said.

"You're only saying that 'cause you can't beat me."

"I can beat you … anytime."

"Not until you read some of the books," Aaron said.

"I got better things to do."

"Hey, guys. Enough bickering."

They sat quietly for a minute or two and then Clay spoke up. "Is George going to take us to see those puppies?"

"Unless he says otherwise. It strikes me he's a man who keeps his promises."

"I hope so," Clay said. "I want to see those puppies."

They turned at the sound of a car in the parking lot and they were surprised when Captain Eddie Bayles stepped out and walked toward them. He was in full uniform, the left side of his chest covered with ribbons, and the eagles on his collar ends flashing in the sunlight.

"Hi," he said as he walked up to the blanket. "I stopped at the house and then decided to check the beach."

Linda stood up. "What brings you out here?"

"I wanted to have a look around again."

"I don't think anything's changed."

He smiled. "No, I suspect it hasn't."

"Was it a bullet hole?" Aaron asked.

"It was, but the question is when it was made. It's possible that the hole might have been made a long time ago."

"I take it you don't think so," Linda said.

"Well, as a matter of fact, I don't." He shook his head. "I was also trying to find George Bean. I checked at the store and the man there told me to ask you. Do you know him?"

"Yes," Linda said. "He's down in Hyannis today."

"Darn the luck. I knew I should have called."

"You sound as if you know him too?"

Aaron and Clay listened to every word.

"We were in the same carrier wing. Then he went down at Iwo and he was listed as missing in action." He looked around at all of them. "Has he told you the story?"

"Story?" Clay's voice betrayed his excitement.

"Well, he managed to crash land his plane and then he slipped off into the jungle. He was pretty banged up but he fought his way back through the Japanese and along the way managed to blow up two ammo dumps and take out several Japanese officers, one of them a colonel, using a captured sniper rifle, before he slipped through their lines and ours and reported in. He'd taken two bullets and some shrapnel in his legs from a grenade and he'd been in the jungle three days and nobody could figure out why he wasn't dead.

"The doctors said it was a miracle that he survived, let alone managed to fight his own private war. The last time I saw him he was wrapped in bandages ready to be shipped home to recover." He shoved his hands into his pockets. "I don't think anybody believed he could have done what he said until we overran the Japanese positions and found the ammo dumps and the dead officers. Up till then all anybody knew about him was that he was one heck of a fighter pilot. He'd had twenty-eight kills. So you can imagine my surprise when I looked at the list of the houses within range of where my plane went down and his name came up."

"Some coincidence," Linda said.

"I thought so myself." He smiled. "I was really looking forward to seeing him again."

She looked down at her watch. "He's expected around four and that's only an hour from now. In fact, we're just about ready to go back to the cottage, so why don't you come with us and I'll make some coffee. George is planning to stop at the cottage on the way to his place."

"Thank you very much," Captain Bayles said. "A cup of coffee would sure hit the spot."

If George had avoided telling war stories, Captain Bayles didn't seem to mind at all. And while they waited in the kitchen, sitting around the big oak table, he told them about the campaign in the Pacific.

He'd just finished when George stepped into the cottage. "I knew I recognized that voice," he said. "Eddie Bayles. Best wingman I ever flew with. Shot three Zeros off my tail in one afternoon. Damn, Eddie, it's good to see you!"

They shook hands, both of them smiling in a way neither of the boys had ever seen, because it is the way men smile at each other who have shared an experience that neither of them should have survived.

"What brings you out here?"

"I was flying the plane that went down."

"I wondered who the pilot was. Even more I wondered why it wasn't in the papers."

"Security. You remember."

"Even so. We're not exactly at war now."

"It's the communists. Everybody's turning over every rock they can find, looking for communists."

"But here? On the Cape? In Eastham? Be a lonely communist who lived out here. Might find some in Provincetown, though."

Linda set a cup of coffee in front of George and refilled Eddie's cup.

Aaron and Clay sat as if they'd been glued to their chairs. You never got a chance to hear stuff like this and they were absorbing the words like empty sponges. And Aaron found himself comparing the two men, weighing one against the other and wondering how his father would have fit in with them. And then, he found out.

"And it's also a pretty strange coincidence that it should happen here, where you live, and it even gets more strange when you discover that Linda is Mrs. Winslow Harrison."

"Yeah," George smiled. "Quite a coincidence."

Captain Bayles looked at Aaron and Clay. "Your dad was the most admired submarine skipper in the whole war. He drove the Japanese Navy absolutely crazy for three years. Guys who sailed with him said it was as if he could hear what the enemy was thinking."

"He played chess," Aaron said.

"Now why doesn't that surprise me?" George said.

"There was no one like him," Eddie said.

"Now tell me," George said, "were you shot down?"

"The Navy is not going to admit it, but I know what happens when you take one in the engine."

"Then what's going on?"

"It feels like a cover-up, but it makes no sense."

"It would have taken one hell of a shot." George looked around at Aaron and Clay. "These guys tell me it was a fifty caliber round?"

"It was."

"Then it had to have come from the target hulk but the thing is, it's an almost impossible shot on a plane at the bottom of a dive. The plane's just moving too fast."

Eddie scratched his head. "You're right. It would be a world record shot. And yet … somebody made it."

"I've been shooting my whole life," George said, "especially at ducks, and the hardest shot is always on ducks dropping down onto the decoys because you have to get the gun barrel under them. It's tough enough with a shotgun, but with a single bullet it's probably impossible."

"Maybe it was a sort of intentional accident," Captain Bayles said. "Maybe the shooter just got lucky. What I mean is, he might have meant to hit the plane, but it still would have taken an incredibly lucky shot. Maybe he's been doing this for a long time and mine was the first plane he hit."

"Why would anyone do that?" Aaron asked, noticing as he spoke, the strange sort of distant look that Captain Bayles cast toward George, and wondering what that meant.

George smiled around at him. "That, of course, is the great question, Aaron." He turned toward Captain Bayles. "Does anyone actually think it could be some crazy communist?"

"You know how intelligence guys are. They never tell anyone anything. But we sent a team in to investigate the target ship and they found nothing."

"I spend a lot of time out there, Eddie, and even from well outside the 'no traffic' zone I've never seen any boat close to the target."

"Well, it had to come from somewhere." Captain Bayles stood up. "I've got to get back to the base," he said. "Thanks for the coffee, Mrs. Harrison, and it was nice seeing you guys again." He laughed. "Just look out for old George here. You can never tell what he'll get up to next."

George laughed and then walked out to the car with his old friend.

"Did you hear that story about George?" Clay asked.

"And what about Dad?" Aaron asked. "That's amazing!"

"Mom, how come you never told us about that?"

"I didn't know about it. Sometimes the military doesn't tell you everything. And your father was too modest to think of himself as a hero. But his boat had the highest number of kills in the sub service."

"Wow!" Aaron sat wide-eyed, wondering whether he was like his father. Would he have the courage to do something like that, to keep going out time after time to face the enemy? Or did stuff like that only happen in wars? "What was Dad like?"

She smiled, only too willing to repeat this information over and over. "He was kind and smart and he believed in truth and justice and honor and he had a will of steel. And he loved to laugh. When we'd go to the movies, and it was a comedy, you could hear him laugh above the whole audience. And when he was home he was always busy fixing things or keeping our old car running. I think everybody liked him but the men always gave him a wide berth."

"What does that mean … a wide berth?" Clay asked.

"Well … let's just say other men seemed to know that he was not someone you messed around with."

"Yeah," Aaron said. "I like that."

21

Secrets From The Barn

In the middle of the night when they knew their mother was asleep, Clay and Aaron crept outside and buried the net, covering it with at least an inch of sand. Then they buried the net wires which led back up to the rope, which in turn, was connected to the concrete block.

They ran the trip wire across the middle of the net and led it back inside the barn up to the hole in the floor of the loft where it was connected through a set of pulleys to a stick. And finally, they tipped the block back out over the hole, balanced it against the stick and connected the trip wire.

"Will it work?" Aaron asked.

"Sure it'll work," Clay said.

"We should have tried it first."

"It'll work."

Aaron glanced up at the concrete block, its pale gray color showing even in the dark of the barn. "How can you be so sure?"

"Don't worry, Aaron. Jeesh!"

"Okay, okay. Let's go to bed."

They crossed the lawn and slipped through the back door, Aaron congratulating himself on having oiled the spring. They made it upstairs without a single squeak from the steps and then climbed into bed and lay in the dark, looking up at the ceiling.

"We'll have to get up very early," Aaron said.

"Why?"

"To make sure we don't catch George. He might want something from the barn and he doesn't know about the trap. We might even catch Mom."

Clay sat up straight. Clearly this was something he hadn't thought of. "How will we get up? We don't have an alarm clock."

Aaron got out of bed, walked to the east window, and raised the heavy shade. Then he swung his bed so that the morning sun would shine directly onto his face. "The sun will wake me," he said.

"Pretty smart," Clay said, "if it works."

"It wouldn't work on you. You sleep like a stone."

"And you don't?"

"Not with the sun in my face. It wakes me right up."

Minutes later Clay was asleep but Aaron lay awake, thinking about the trap, going over the wires and ropes and wondering how hard you'd have to jerk the trip wire. He wished they'd had time to try it, but they'd barely had time to get everything in place as it was. Now all he had to do was wake up early enough to disarm it.

And then, as his mind drifted from thought to thought and he felt sleep edging closer he suddenly came wide awake. Why had Captain Bayles looked at George in that funny way? Did he think George had something to do with shooting down his plane? Why would he think that? Because George could shoot ducks? What sense would that make? Unless there was something about George they didn't know. But what could it be? He stared up into the dark, trying to imagine what might have happened to him but nothing he thought of fit George Bean. And then he remembered the part of Captain Bayles's story about George killing those Jap officers with a sniper rifle. But as good a shot as it would have taken, it wouldn't have been anything like trying to hit an airplane with a single bullet. And then he wondered again about Mrs. Coleman. All along he had thought her son must have killed her but maybe it was someone else. But who? And why? Why did anyone kill anyone else? Too many questions. Way too many questions.

He rolled onto his side, and then rolled onto his other side and then finally turned onto his back again because that way he could hear with both ears.

The sun blasted through the window like a bright yellow cannon but it had absolutely no effect on Aaron. He lay sleeping on his stomach, absolutely still, breathing slowly and deeply as the sun rose higher and higher, climbing past the halfway point of his window and then to the top of the frame. Still he slept.

An hour or so later Clay woke up, pulled on his shorts and sneaks, and walked downstairs and outside to take a leak. He thought about checking the trap but there wouldn't be anything in it or Aaron would have gotten him up. This time he walked right to the outhouse, opened the door and stepped in, closing the door behind him. He was so busy thinking about the trap that he never once thought about spiders until he had finished and stepped outside. He grinned to himself. Maybe spiders were behind him now.

He took a step and then stopped, holding his breath and listening. In the distance he could hear crows and gulls and the chirping of a bird he didn't recognize, and then he heard something else. It was like someone breathing very slowly and it seemed to be coming from the lower level of the barn. He took a deep breath. If you could get over spiders, then you could get over something like this, especially since he knew it was nothing but his imagination running wild.

He walked into the house, got the key to the padlock, and headed for the boat doors in the back of the barn. He opened the lock, pulled back the door, stepped inside, and stopped. It wasn't a matter of hearing something now. The hair on the back of his neck suddenly stood up and he shivered but still, he didn't run. Why should he run? He was Clay Harrison and his father had been a great hero. He took another step into the damp basement, looking around, scanning rapidly from side to side and up and down. The air felt heavy and when he looked through to the end wall and the neatly laid-up stones the air seemed wavy the same way it did over hot pavement.

His feet felt heavy and yet he managed to take another

step closer to the wall. Then he took another and another and stopped. There was something odd about that wall. Most of the stones were the same color but there was one patch where they were lighter and drier looking. He stepped closer and closer and the air grew steadily heavier and now it was hard to breath. He was shaking all over as he stopped at the wall, reached out, grabbed hold of one of the light colored stones and then stopped. "Okay," he said, "here goes nothing," and he pulled the stone out of the wall.

A rush of air came from the hole left by the stone and it smelled very old and moldy and it was almost as if he could see it in the air around him. And then it was gone. Well, at lest there aren't any spiders, he thought, and he pulled away another stone. Now the air seemed to vibrate, making a soft rattling sound, but still Clay held firm, determined now to find out what lay behind this wall.

Stone by stone he kept at it until he had opened a space a couple of feet tall and four feet long. Now, as he looked into the hole he could see something inside. It looked like a mummy wrapped in rotted cloth. That's when he headed for high ground, running so fast as he came out of the barn, he only hit the ground about every third step.

And because he was looking over his shoulder he ran smack into Aaron and both of them tumbled over the grass.

"What's the matter with you?" Aaron hollered. "Don't you know enough to look where you're going?"

Clay just sat in the grass, staring at the open lower door of the barn and Aaron wondered if maybe he'd gotten hurt in the collision. "Hey, you okay?"

"Did we catch him?" Clay shook his head. "I hope we

caught him, I really hope we caught him ..."

"What are you talking about?"

"In the trap! Did we catch him?"

"No. And we're pretty lucky too because I never did wake up. I just now disarmed it and then I heard something in the lower part of the barn and then next thing I know I'm being used for target practice in a bowling alley." He stood up slowly. "What was it? The wolf spider?"

Clay grinned. "No. Much scarier than a spider. You wanna see?"

"Sure?"

"Com'on, I'll show you."

But at the door he stopped and pointed. "It's back there in that hole."

"Aren't you coming?"

Clay looked around the inside of the building and he even sniffed the air. "Do you smell anything?"

"Just the mildew."

"Maybe it's gone."

"What's gone?"

"The ghost."

Aaron laughed. "You're joking, right? A ghost?"

"Yeah, well you wouldn't have thought it was so funny a few minutes ago. And if you're so brave just walk back to that hole and have a look."

Aaron walked to the back of the barn and looked into the hole.

"Now," Clay called, "is that what I think it is?"

"Wow," Aaron said. "It looks like a body all wrapped up like a mummy!"

"Yeah, and when I pulled the rocks away something came out of there!"

"We better go get Mom," Aaron said , backing away from the hole. "This place has got bodies everywhere."

"I don't even wanna think about that!" Clay said.

"Damn, Clay. I can't believe how brave you were, just walking up there and pulling out the stones! I couldn't have done that!"

And if that made Clay feel a good deal better, he still wasn't going back into the barn. "Hey," he said, "you just swore! We're not supposed to swear."

"I know, I know. Just don't tell Mom, okay?"

"Can I swear too?"

"Sure, go ahead. Knock yourself out!"

"What are you mad about?"

"Nothing. Right now we need to go get George! He's got a phone!"

Back in the barn, with the police on their way, George looked into the hole with his big spotlight. "Unless I miss my guess, it looks like you've found another of the missing Colemans," he said. "Now, I wonder if there isn't at least one more here somewhere."

"I think I know," Aaron said, "what the names mean."

"The names?" his mother asked.

"The White Knight and the Black Queen and the Queen's Pawn."

George looked around. "The queen's pawn? Where did that come from?"

"When we were digging clams the other day we found an old boat mostly buried in the mud and it had a name on the back."

"*The Queen's Pawn,*" George said.

"Right," Aaron said. "So I think that Paul Coleman was the white knight and the black queen was Mrs. Coleman and the box was supposed to be her coffin, and the queen's pawn was either the father or the brother."

"Chess pieces," George said. "Of course."

"What made me think of it was the chess game you were playing ... where you captured the black queen with the white knight."

"Only I lost the knight. In fact, I still haven't figured out how to make that move without losing the knight. Only I was using the black knight. I always play the black pieces when I can." He shook his head and looked around at Linda. "I'm feeling pretty awful about this," he said. "I rent you the place for a nice quiet vacation and then bodies start turning up like schools of blues. So I've got a proposition for you. Why don't you stay with me for the rest of your vacation? I've got rooms enough and I think we'd have a great time. What's more, I'm going to refund your rent. It's the least I could do."

"Mom?" Clay asked, "is that okay?"

Aaron wasn't sure what to say.

"It's a terrible imposition," Linda said.

"Not at all," George said. "In fact it would be my pleasure." He grinned. "Captain's too."

She frowned. "I really don't see how we could do that, George. I mean, it just wouldn't be appropriate."

"Mom!" Clay said, "forget about that stuff! George says it's okay and think of all the fun we'll have!" He looked down.

"Besides this place is too scary now."

And that Aaron could agree on, but what he really wanted now was just to go home, to get away from all this because it had gotten much too complicated. And yet there was no way he could say that. All he could do was go along.

Linda looked carefully at her two sons and then smiled up at George. "Aaron?"

"I agree with Clay," he said.

"Well, it looks as if propriety is not a big issue in this session of Congress. But only if you're absolutely certain. I mean, you've done so much already."

"No imposition at all."

"Can we go fishing again?" Clay asked.

"Sure. I just want you to feel at home." He looked around at the basement walls and shook his head. "Gonna be hard to feel at home around here," he said. "Especially since they'll most likely send a crew in to tear this place apart on the chance that there is another body."

"There is," Clay said.

Everyone looked at him.

"How do you know there is?" Aaron asked. "Nobody knows stuff like that."

"Yeah, well how do you think I found this one? Why did I start pulling stones out of the wall, huh?"

"Now there's a question that'll be hard to answer," George said.

"How *did* you know to do that?" Linda asked.

For an instant he thought about trying to explain, but decided that it'd just make him look foolish. No. There was another way. "The rocks were a different color." He pointed to the wall. "Most of them are still there, see? But they aren't fitted into the darker rocks very well and if you look at the rest of the wall you can see how they all overlap." He looked down and then up. What he'd said was true enough but he wondered if they would buy it. He thought about the air and how heavy and wavy it had seemed and how hard it had been to breathe and how the air had rushed out at him after he pulled away the first stone.

"Tell them about the ghost," Aaron said.

"Shut up, Aaron!"

"Did you see it?" George asked.

He shook his head. "It was like something in the air, something heavy and damp and then it was gone. I felt it before we found Mrs. Coleman too."

"Do you feel it now?" George asked.

Clay nodded. "But not as strong. I think it's upstairs."

"Well, let's go have a look," George said.

They climbed the stairs into the main body of the barn and at first Clay just stood there looking around. Nothing seemed out of place and even the big wolf spider put in an appearance, dancing down the work bench to disappear in the same spot it always did.

Clay walked down the aisle to the front of the barn and then turned and walked back up the far aisle and then stopped. "It could be anywhere," he said.

"Are you sure there's something here?" his mother asked.

"Pretty sure." But now he wasn't at all sure.

"Should we keep searching?" George asked.

"We don't need to," Aaron said and pointed to a spot in the stacked lobster traps. "It's right in there."

George and Clay came around the pile and began pulling it apart. In the middle they found a coffin and on the lid was painted, "The Black King."

"Well, look at that," George said.

Clay stared at his brother and then shook his head and then shook his head again. "How did you know?"

Aaron touched the end of his nose. "I could smell it," he said. "I told you I can smell stuff."

"Well, how about that," George said. "You two guys make one heck of a team." He walked to the bench, picked up a pry bar, forced it under the edge of the cover with a hammer, and pulled upward. Bit by bit the top came loose and finally he slipped it off to one side. The cloth the body had been wrapped in had rotted and fallen away over the years and what they saw was a mummified skeleton much like Mrs. Coleman's ... except that this one had a bullet hole in the middle of its forehead.

"I'd guess they won't have much trouble figuring out what killed this fellow," George said.

Aaron looked at the skeleton and suddenly he saw it as just that, a skeleton, something every human had. He looked at the way the bones went together and he began to wonder where the muscles would have been.

"There aren't any more," Clay said.

"How long have you known about this?" Linda asked.

"From the first morning, but it wasn't always very strong." He smiled. "It's gone now."

"Did this ever happen before?" George asked.

Clay shook his head. "Never. Not even in graveyards. Just here."

"Clay, you're as brave as Dad was," Aaron said. "You walked right into the barn and pulled those stones away. Not me. I'd have run like a rabbit." He shivered. "I don't even like to say the word ghost."

"Do you think that's what it was? A ghost?"

"No," George said. "At least not what people think of as ghosts. But as to what you felt, Clay, I don't think anyone knows what causes that."

"You weren't even scared, were you?" Linda asked.

He shook his head. "Of course I was, Mom. If I hadn't just gone to the outhouse, I'd have peed my pants."

They all laughed and then turned toward the front of the barn as they heard the cars pulling in. "I think the law has arrived," George said. "Guess we'll have them start with the upstairs cadaver."

Sgt. Oberlin led the way. "Damn, George," he said, "this place is turning out to be a regular burying ground."

"Harry on his way?" George asked.

"Be here any minute. Now, what have we got here?"

"Got one back there and another downstairs and I think that about takes care of the Coleman family."

They heard another car pull in and Harry Stout climbed out of his car and walked into the barn.

Aaron saw George glance up at the hole in the ceiling where the big concrete block sat just out of sight, but he said nothing about it, instead turning to their mother. "Why don't you guys get packed and when I've finished here we'll go up to the house and settle in."

"You're sure about this," Linda said.

"Wouldn't have offered, if I weren't." He smiled around

at Aaron and then looked back at Linda. "Apart from all the dead people turning up, this is the most fun I've had in a long, long time."

From his mother's smile, Aaron wondered how long it would be before they moved to Cape Cod.

Upstairs, as they packed their stuff into suitcases, Aaron looked over at Clay. "He saw the hole in the floor."

"Uh-oh."

"Yeah. It won't take him long to figure it out, I don't think."

"Drat!" Clay said. "That was a really neat trap. And it would have worked if he'd shown up."

"The crummy thing is that now we'll be up at George's and we won't have a chance to set it again."

"Do you think he'll come back?"

"He has to. He has to know what we found in the barn."

"The bodies."

"Right."

Clay shook his head. "Wouldn't he figure that out?"

"If it were you, wouldn't you want to be sure?"

"No. I'd just run. Nobody even knows he's alive."

"Except maybe us. We've seen him, you know."

"If that was him."

"I think it was." He lowered the lid on his suitcase and closed the two silvery latches.

Suddenly Clay got it. "You mean he might come after us, don't you?"

"I'll feel much better at George's, especially with Captain there on the porch. Nobody will get close to the house without him barking."

Clay's eyes widened and than grew larger still. "Do you think he's going to try to kill us?"

"He has to."

"Are you gonna tell George?" Clay asked

"I don't know."

"You gotta tell him, Aaron. Look, I told him about the ghost and he didn't laugh at all and I never expected an adult to believe something like that."

"Yeah, me either."

"So, you'll tell him."

"But what if I'm wrong? What if the guy I saw isn't Paul Coleman? I don't wanna look stupid."

"But what if it is him?"

"You think it's better to look stupid, huh?"

"You have to take the chance."

"Because if I don't say anything then there's no way to be ready."

"Be prepared, just like the Boy Scouts say."

"Okay, I'll tell George."

"Good." Clay pushed down the top of his suitcase, but it didn't want to close. "Stupid thing!"

"Let me help," Aaron said and he came around the bed and sat on the suitcase, forcing the lid down so Clay could close the latches.

"Thanks," Clay said. Suddenly he grinned. "Are you gonna like living on Cape Cod?"

"What?"

"I asked you if you are gonna like living here? 'Cause I'm gonna like it a lot."

"You really think that's gonna happen, don't you? You

really think Mom's gonna marry George?"

"Of course she is."

"But we've only known him three weeks!" Aaron said. "I think it's supposed to take longer than that."

"Okay, I admit I don't know anything about stuff like this, but they spend a lot of time looking at each other the way people do in those drippy movies, so I figure that's what's up."

"Yeah, I've noticed that too."

"Don't you want Mom to be happy?"

"It's got nothing to do with that."

"Don't you like George?"

"I like George just fine. In fact, I like him a lot. I just don't know whether ..."

"Whether what?"

"It means a lot of changes, Clay."

"Yeah, instead of being stuck in boring old Chesterfield, we get to go fishing and dig clams and learn how to shoot and hunt and how to run a boat and have dogs and you'll get someone to play chess with and Mom gets someone to talk to, right?"

Aaron laughed. "True enough."

"He'll make a great stepdad," Clay said.

"It just seems like a big change all at once. And it's ... it's happening so fast."

"Okay, look, Aaron. Don't say anything one way or another until you have to. Mom already knows how I feel."

Aaron grinned. "Yeah, you told me. I still don't believe you said that."

"I haven't changed my mind either."

22

A Package Neatly Wrapped

Aaron had to admit that from the time they got to George's house it felt like home. He could not find any other way to describe it. Mom seemed especially relaxed and Clay, well, Clay spent as much time as he could with Captain, having him fetch and then just petting him and talking to him as if he were an old friend.

At lunch George asked them whether they'd like to go for blues again and Aaron discovered that he was every bit as excited about fishing as his brother. And then he took himself out to watch the chickens and the big rooster, wondering why they interested him, but mostly not thinking about that so much as the contrast between the peaceful sounds the hens made as they went pecking about and the clearly warlike strutting of the rooster. He was a fine looking bird with his reddish feathers and his glossy green tail, but it was the bright yellow eyes that most held his attention. They never strayed, but stayed fixed on the large animal that he saw as a threat to his hens. As he watched him, Aaron began to wonder whether in some way he reflected human behavior, and he'd just gotten into that thought when George came up behind him.

"You okay?" George asked.

"Sure, fine."

"Funny, I got the idea you were worrying something."

"Well, maybe, but it's nothing." Now was the time to tell him and yet he could feel himself wanting to hold back.

George stood with his hands pressed against the chicken wire, his body arched away, looking in at the rooster. "Now, that is one aggressive bird," he said. "You see that little door on the front of the chicken house? I had to put that there so I could keep the rooster outside when I go to gather the eggs. Once, before the door was there, he caught me inside and he flew up and drove those big spurs on the insides of his legs right through a rubber boot.

"But I had to put the door on at night because that's the only time he sits still. Even then he kept banging against the door as I tried to screw the hinges on. It was pretty funny."

"Why do you have wire on top of the pen?" Aaron asked. "They can't fly, can they?"

"It's to keep the hawks out. Everything wants to eat chickens. On the ground there are possums and raccoons, even stray dogs. From the air they have to worry about the hawks. But that rooster is one amazing bird. Before I put the wire over the top a big red tailed hawk dropped in and grabbed one of my pullets and that old rooster piled into the hawk, forced him to drop the pullet, and drove him off. Then, another time a raccoon got into the hen house at night and that rooster bailed into the coon and by the time I got here with the light, the coon was gone, but you could see raccoon blood on the roster's spurs for half an inch."

He shook his head. "He's always on guard, always ready to protect his flock and he'll attack anything."

"He sure looks mean," Aaron said.

"But he isn't, really, not the way people can be mean, I don't think. It seems to me he's just doing what he's meant to do."

"Is that true with most animals?"

"Yup, I think it is."

"But not with people?"

"Oh?" George looked around at him.

"Well, like you said, people can be mean for almost no reason."

"Or maybe they have a reason. The problem with humans is that you can never see that coming."

"It would be easier if I were a rooster, I think."

"Perhaps, but look at him, always alert, always ready to fight. Might be kind of a hard way to live your life. Of course, for the rooster, there is no choice. He's been genetically programmed to do what he does."

"How can you know what you're supposed to do?"

"Probably we do know, at least deep down inside, but so many other things happen that we lose sight of it. Sometimes we simply lack the courage to act. Sometimes ... well, sometimes other things hold us back, things we can't even put a name to. There is no right way or wrong way. In the end we follow our instincts."

"Or other people take over and tell us what to do."

"Like parents and teachers."

Aaron grinned. "Sure."

"Seems like a bad idea, doesn't it?"

"It does to me."

"Always did to me too. I think Dad and I still get along because we spent so much time away from home. He's a pretty bossy guy. Sea captains don't ask, they give orders because that's what captains do."

Aaron nodded. "I hate taking orders."

"You're supposed to hate it. But sometimes there's no other way."

"Like in the service."

"Exactly."

"I can see that all right. But what about parents?"

"I think it comes down to this. Parents have to make sure their kids know right from wrong and how to avoid danger. Of course, I never met a kid who thought that was a good idea, but it doesn't matter, because parents have to make sure their kids know."

"You mean like what to do in a boat, for example?"

"Yup. And a lot of other things. Look at it from your mom's point of view. You guys are the most important thing in the world to her, so she has to do everything she can to make sure you grow up safely. And she's done a heck of a job, I think." He laughed. "And she doesn't even boss you guys around much."

Aaron smiled. "It doesn't seem that way."

"It never does."

"There was something I wanted to talk to you about."

George nodded.

"The man I told you about. What if he's Paul Coleman? I mean, if he is, then Clay and I are the only ones who can connect him to the cottage because we saw him when he was watching us and he knows we saw him."

"You think maybe he'll try something?"

"He might."

"He might at that. Anybody who would murder his whole family is a pretty desperate man." He let go of the wire and stood up, shoving his hands into his pockets. "I hadn't thought about that. I'm glad you mentioned it."

"Do you think it could be true?"

"I don't see why not, but in any case, it's always better to be prepared, isn't it? Just look at that rooster: always ready, always prepared. How else can he defend his flock?"

Aaron said nothing.

"And now it's time to grab the equipment and see if we can find some bluefish."

They went out to the same spot once again, only now the wind had begun to kick up out of the southwest and it was a rougher ride and slower, because with the waves running three and four feet, George had to run at half throttle to keep the boat from pounding back down onto the water. Even without that, it was a wild ride.

They made two passes up through the rip without a fish and then the third time through, George zig-zagged the course of the boat and almost immediately they began to pick up fish, none of the big fifteen-pounders they had caught before but instead, fish in the eight-pound class. And while the bigger fish wore you down more, just because they were heavier, these fish seemed to fight harder, even smashing through the surface to walk on their tails as they tried to shake the hook loose.

But this school quit much sooner. And after they had caught a couple of fish apiece, the blues simply disappeared and no matter what George tried, they got no more hits. Still they kept at it, until finally, after about the fifteenth run up through the rip, George reeled in his line. "Okay, that's it," he said. "School's moved."

"Won't they come back?" Clay asked.

"Not likely. Blues are always moving, looking for more feed. Very hungry fish."

Aaron and Clay reeled in and George turned the boat for home.

"Who cares," Clay said. "We got plenty of fish."

They finished the afternoon with a swim in the salt water and a dip in the pond and then headed back to the house for a dinner of blues and cherrystones and a big salad from George's garden.

And after dinner, as they were cleaning up, George asked them to explain again what they had seen when Eddie Bayles's plane went down.

George nodded as he listened to their explanations. "How close together were the planes when they came in? What I mean is, were they closer the second time than the first?"

"A lot closer," Clay said.

"They were right on each other's tail!" Aaron added

quickly. "I thought they might hit each other."

George grinned. "Hot shot pilots … what would you say, fifty yards?"

"How far is that?" Clay asked.

George pointed out the window to a tree on the lawn. "From here to that tree."

"Closer," Aaron said. "A lot closer."

Clay agreed.

Without a word George turned and walked out into the west wing of the house where he had his office, and when he came back he had a book, a pad of paper, a ruler, a protractor and a slide rule, and he sat down at the table and began digging through the book, writing down numbers and working out the calculations on his slide rule. Then he began making lines on the paper.

Suddenly he smiled and sat up. "Well, I think that mystery is solved. I know how Eddie got shot down."

"How?" Linda asked as she sat down at the table.

"It was a ricochet … a round from the plane behind him. The bullets travel a lot faster than the planes and a round from the plane behind hit the ship and deflected upward and into his engine. Here," he pointed to the lines on the paper, "you can see how it would work."

Linda looked at the lines and shook her head. "I'll take your word for it."

Aaron smiled and the last doubt he'd had about George disappeared.

Clay looked down at the lines on the paper and then smiled again. "Would you show me how to do that sometime?"

"Sure," George said.

He reached into his shirt pocket and took out a card. "Why don't you get the Monopoly board set up and I'll go call Eddie. I hope you guys are ready to lose," he said, "'cause I'm a devilish good Monopoly player."

They all laughed.

"What did Captain Bayles say?" Linda asked as George came back.

"He'll check the hole in the cowling tomorrow. I told him to look for even the least evidence that the bullet came in at an angle. It shouldn't be too hard to spot."

It was a wild Monopoly game, with everyone whooping and hollering and after two hours it came to a standoff. The properties were too scattered and nobody was willing to make a deal. George tried to wheedle them into making a trade, but Aaron said it clearly. "Why should I take the risk? I can't win if I don't, but I can't lose either."

George laughed. "Precisely my way of thinking," he said. Then he stood up and stretched.

"I've got to go check the boat," he said. "See you guys in the morning."

They walked up to the big room they shared overlooking the water. They climbed into bed and Linda sat near by in a rocking chair. "I need to talk to you guys about something," she said. "We've never talked before about the possibility of a stepfather."

"You mean George?" Clay said.

"I know we haven't known him very long," she said. "But … well, we seem to like each other quite a lot, well … maybe a good deal more than that … and, well, he's asked me to marry him. I said I had to talk to you guys first."

"I already told you, Mom. Marry him," Clay said.

"Would we live here?" Aaron asked.

"We would, and I know it means moving away from your friends and all."

"So what," Clay said. "We'd have dogs and we'd get to fish and hunt and go out in boats and all kinds of neat stuff."

Linda smiled. "And more Monopoly games and chess."

Aaron had known it was coming, of course, but now that it was here ... the idea still made him uneasy and yet he couldn't think why.

"It won't change our family," Linda said, "but it will make a lot of things possible. I won't have to work, unless I want to, and I don't. So I'd be around more. George is going to open a law office and I think he knows nearly everyone on the Cape. He might even go into politics."

"What kind of politics?" Aaron asked.

"He said some men want him to run for Congress."

Aaron's eyebrows shot up. "Like in Washington?"

"Uh-huh. But not for several years yet, anyway. Not until the present Congressman retires."

"Do you really, really like him, Mom?" Aaron asked.

"I do, Aaron," she said.

"Then it's okay with me too. Especially now."

"Why now?" his mother asked.

"Because now I know he didn't shoot down the plane."

"What? You thought he did that? How could you think such a thing?"

"Because he's got all those guns and he can really shoot and he spends a lot of time out in his boat. It wasn't that I thought he did it so much as I thought he could have done it. But then he showed us how it happened."

"Wow," Clay said. "I never thought about that."

"When would we move?" Aaron asked.

"I don't know for sure. Probably before Thanksgiving."

"Why not right away?" Clay asked. "Then we could start school here."

"Aaron?"

He smiled. "Clay's right. The sooner the better."

"I'll talk to George." She smiled at her sons. "Thanks, guys, I think this is going to work out just fine."

"We do too, Mom," Aaron said. "We're getting to where it will be good to have a man around too."

She smiled. "You guys do say some amazing things."

In the morning, very early in the morning, in the dark before the sun had even touched the horizon, suddenly George went from room to room , getting them up and telling them he had something to show them. Half-asleep they all tumbled out to the car and George drove them down to the cottage. When they pulled in and stopped, they couldn't believe their eyes.

There, neatly bagged, and hanging in the fish net was a short man with a full gray beard, cursing and swearing and struggling but there was no way he could escape the net.

"You set the trap!" Aaron shouted. "And it worked!"

"You guys built a terrific trap," George said. "I couldn't have built a better one myself."

"Aaron said he thought you'd seen it," Clay said.

"I saw the hole in the barn ceiling and when I came down

to see to the boat I checked it out. At first I couldn't figure out why you went to so much trouble and then I noticed the marks on the padlock where somebody had tried to saw it through. So, I figured I'd … give it a try."

"And it worked!" Clay shouted.

"Are you going to let him down?" Linda asked. "He doesn't look very comfortable."

"The police are on their way. I think Mr. Coleman is going to have a lot of explaining to do."

"What do you think he wanted in the barn?" Clay asked.

"Now that's a good question," George said. "And why did he wait until I'd locked it up to come after it?"

"I know what he was after," Aaron said. "He was going to get rid of the other bodies."

"Good guess," George said. "A very good guess."

"I've got a question," Clay said. "Will we still call you George after you and Mom get married?"

George laughed. "Of course," he said. "You've only got one dad. I'm just filling in because he can't be here."

And that, Aaron thought, was the perfect answer.